Lost... and Never Found II

Lost... and Never Found II

Anita Larsen

SCHOLASTIC INC.
New York Toronto London Auckland Sydney

ISBN 0-590-43878-6

12 11 10 9 8 7 6 5 4 3 2 1   1 2 3 4 5 6/9

Printed in the U.S.A.   01

First Scholastic printing, January 1991

Contents

Introduction

An estimated ten million persons are reported missing each year in the United States. There are three to four times that many worldwide. These are big numbers.

The first question that occurs to those they left behind is, What happened to them? The second question is usually, Why? In some cases that question is easier to answer than the first.

There are several explanations for the disappearance of most missing persons. The first is that they simply want out. They haven't, for one reason or another, wanted to continue being who they are or where they are any longer, so they leave. Many of the approximately 600,000 teenagers who run away every year do so for this reason.

Another major reason people vanish is amnesia — a sudden loss of memory. These missing persons simply don't remember that they have already built a life somewhere, so they don't realize they are missing. There is another large group of missing persons who vanish because they have been kidnapped.

Cases of missing persons have different causes, but most of them have something in common. Usually the lost people are found. Their cases are solved; their case files are stamped CLOSED. In fact, 95 percent of all missing persons cases *are* solved. Most of the missing turn up by themselves sooner or later. Most of those who don't are found by federal, state, or local officials.

Every major city in the world has a missing persons bureau on its police force; the world's largest is the Central Tracing Agency in Geneva. National social and religious organizations also help trace missing persons. The Salvation Army, for example, operates a Missing Persons Locater Service in the United States and in eighty-six other countries. The service is available to the public.

But it is the inexplicably missing that intrigue us. For that handful of people who slip through the cracks, who seemingly vanish into thin air, there are nagging questions. After searchers fail comes a haunted oblivion for these missing persons. They are lost . . . and never found.

There are no solid answers to any of the questions about their fate, and there probably never will be. The mysterious stories of some of these people are in this book.

Didirici

It is 1815.

This year *Grimm's Fairy Tales* will be published in Germany. And this year an inmate in a grim German prison will disappear in a way that seems like a fairy tale.

Watch as it happens:

A line of men shuffles into the yard from their cells in the Wiechselmunde, a fortress prison in Prussia, now a part of Germany. The men have been brought out for exercise.

The prisoners may be thinking about the rushing waters in the free-flowing Vistula River, on whose banks the prison sits. They may be wondering what is going on in Danzig, the city outside the twenty-foot-high stone prison walls. But neither river nor city are within the reach of these men.

The prisoners are manacled at hands and feet. They are linked together by chains. Even though there is little chance any one of them could dash away in a mad escape attempt, all of them can see the armed guards watching them closely. The line of chained and manacled prisoners clanks around the yard, each one following the one ahead, each one followed by the one behind.

One of the prisoners is a man called Didirici. He has occupied cell number 80 in this prison since he was exposed as an impersonator. He had pretended to be his master, Captain Fritz Alswanger.

Didirici was valet to the Prussian officer in 1811, when the captain died of apoplexy, a sudden blood clot in the brain. After Captain Alswanger died, Didirici took over his master's name and continued to draw his pay. He cut a fine figure and even attracted the interest of several aristocratic ladies.

Life had been good then. But now Didirici is reduced to trudging around the prison yard in chains.

Around and around the line of prisoners shuffles. Perhaps some of them think of escape, but there is no escape.

Or is there?

Today, Didirici will find a way.

Under the gaze of guards and fellow inmates, his body begins to fade. The outlines of his body grow dimmer and dimmer, until finally, he evaporates completely.

He leaves behind empty manacles and a heap of limp chains.

He also leaves behind a crowd of gaping witnesses — astonished guards and inmates, who blink and ask one another, "What happened to Didirici? Where did he go?"

When Didirici's vanishing act was reported to officials, they echoed those questions. The questions are still unanswered. No one knows for sure what happened to Didirici — except that he escaped.

Perhaps the most astonishing feature of Didirici's disappearance isn't that he vanished in such an eerie way. Perhaps it is that Didirici is not the *only* person ever to vanish like that.

As reported in *Lost . . . and Never Found*, a young Alabama farmer named Orion Williamson also vanished mysteriously, in 1854. But there was a difference between the two strange disappearances. Williamson "blinked" out. One minute he was there; the next he wasn't.

Can scientists who studied the Williamson case offer any insight into what happened to Didirici?

One theory concerning Williamson was that he had walked into a "void spot of universal ether," a meandering and momentary spot that destroys whatever it touches. It strikes, then leaves. Another theory held that Williamson had walked into a "magnetic field" from which he was hurled into another dimension, the fourth dimension.

Could either of these theories explain what had happened to Didirici?

Perhaps. Perhaps not. No one knows exactly what happened to him in that grim prison yard that day, but it's clear he never returned to cell number 80.

He was lost . . . and never found.

Helen Brach

There's much confusion over who was the last person to see Helen Brach before she disappeared in mid-February 1977.

There's an equal amount of confusion over the exact date of her disappearance.

Nobody can even be positive about who the last person was to *hear* her voice on the phone.

Or when.

And Helen Brach's bizarre disappearance got still more confusing as time went on. Witnesses' stories kept shifting. These witnesses contradicted one another and confounded themselves.

As the widow of Frank Brach, one of the three founders of E. J. Brach & Sons candy company of Chicago, Illinois, Helen Brach left behind $21 million. Some of the confusion about her disappearance was caused by so much money at stake. If she was dead, the trust department of the Continental Bank would legally be able to do what it wanted with her fortune. If she was simply missing, her accountant, Everett Moore, would legally have control.

The other cause for confusion was Brach's friends. Though the missing woman had heaps of money, she had few close friends. And some of the ones she did have seemed intent on destroying clues that might have led to finding her.

Investigators could, however, follow a "paper trail" to discover the pattern of Brach's last days.

Some of her final days — the ones we can be sure of — were spent in Rochester, Minnesota. She had checked into the renowned Mayo Clinic. Helen Brach was sixty-five, and she was worried about her health. She was afraid she might be getting arthritis. She went to Rochester to get a medical exam.

Many people go to this clinic — Presidents, celebrities whose names are household words, ordinary people. All of the patients have one thing in common, though. They have to make appointments months in advance.

But Helen Brach didn't have to wait. One of her friends, Richard Bailey, wrangled an appointment for her. Bailey had dated Brach for four years and had sold her nine racehorses worth some $200,000. He seems to have known someone at the hospital who was able to give Brach an appointment that suited her schedule.

That schedule was tight. Brach had recently purchased an expensive condominium in Ft. Lauderdale, Florida. She'd made an appointment with an attorney there for the week after she left the clinic to attend to the final details of the purchase.

She was eager to decorate the condo, too. In fact, she may have planned never to return north to live once she arrived in Florida.

In Rochester, Helen Brach stayed where many Mayo Clinic outpatients and family members stay, the Kahler Hotel. The hotel was across the street from the clinic, connected to it by a tunnel. The tunnel helped visitors avoid the harsh winter weather in Rochester. It also housed an arcade of specialty shops where visitors could buy gifts and other items they needed during their stay.

One clue in Brach's paper trail was from a shop in that underground arcade. Other clues surfaced from Brach's telephone use. Telephone company records for February 17, 1977, show that she called several people from her hotel room on that fateful Thursday morning.

About 10:00 A.M., she called a former Brach company employee, now a friend, in Florida. The friend and his wife usually met Brach at the airport when she flew down to visit. Brach told them she wouldn't be arriving in Florida on Monday, February 21, as she had planned. She would have to change an appointment with her attorney and also one she'd made with a beautician. Brach said she would be arriving soon, but she didn't know exactly when. She'd let them know.

Brach hung up and placed her final call from Rochester at about 10:30 A.M. This time she called Jack Matlick. Matlick was caretaker of Brach's mansion in Glenview, a suburb of Chicago. He lived there when she was traveling or living in another of her homes. When she was in Glenview, he would return to his own family, who lived in yet another house Brach owned. Matlick had worked for the Brach family for nearly twenty years, ever since Frank Brach hired him. Helen fired Matlick after her husband died, then rehired him a couple of months later when he couldn't find another job.

Telephone records show that Brach had talked with Matlick many times during her four-day stay in Rochester. Her last call to him was the longest — forty-five minutes. Since Brach was thinking about moving from the Chicago area permanently, her conversation with Matlick may have been about that. He may have learned that in the future his job would be vastly different from what it was now. He may have learned he wouldn't have a job.

The paper trail continues with checks. After she finished talking with Matlick, Helen Brach checked out of the Kahler Hotel. She paid her bill with a personal check, number 4921. She left her bag with a clerk there, then went across the street to the Mayo Clinic. She read the medical report that declared her healthy and listened to a doctor lecture her about getting some exercise and losing a few pounds. She paid her bill at the hospital with check number 4922.

From there the paper trail leads to a bath shop in the tunnel connecting the clinic and the hotel. Brach bought a set of towels and a matching alabaster-colored soap dish and powder box. They

9

cost $41, which she charged to her American Express card.

Brach asked the salesclerk to mail the things to her new home in Florida. The salesclerk reported later that Helen Brach seemed to be in a good mood that Thursday. She was wearing a full-length mink coat, and her red hair was braided and pinned up in its usual style.

Sometimes Brach would fool those who didn't recognize her with a dark brunette or platinum-blonde wig. Today she hadn't been trying to fool anyone.

She told the clerk about her clean bill of health from the clinic and her eagerness to furnish her Florida condo. She was in a hurry, she said, because the caretaker was waiting for her. Later the clerk said she didn't know if he was waiting for her outside the shop, somewhere in Rochester, at O'Hare Airport in Chicago, in the Glenview house, or in Florida.

That salesclerk was one of the last people to see Helen Brach — alive or dead. After Brach left the bath shop, nothing about her movements is certain.

She *may* have gone back to the hotel to pick up her Samsonite bag. She *may* have caught a cab to the Rochester airport. A cab driver later told a detective that he had taken a woman matching Brach's description there that afternoon.

She *may* have flown to O'Hare. Helen Brach, or someone holding her ticket, took a Northwest Airline flight to Chicago that afternoon. None of the members of the flight crew, however, remembered seeing her on board the plane.

Once in Chicago, Matlick *may* have picked her up and driven her home to Glenview.

Once there, Brach *may* have typed and signed several more checks. Two of these checks were numbered 4924 and 4925, and they were dated 2/17/77. At least six more typed checks shared that date, but they were taken from another packet of checks and were numbered 4976 through 4981.

Altogether the checks totaled $15,000. Matlick said he watched his employer sign them on Sunday, February 20. Most of that $15,000 went to him, a total of $12,100. The checks were paid for strange reasons — unusual bonuses, erratic car purchases, and so on. The signature on these checks looked different. Matlick said that was because Brach's right wrist had been injured when a trunk lid fell on it while she was packing clothes for her trip to Florida.

Later Matlick had another explanation for the signatures. Brach's wrist had been injured by a trunk lid while she was packing quilts.

And even later, experts from the Northern Illinois Crime Lab declared the checks were forgeries. They also found that Matlick himself hadn't signed them.

Then who had?

No one knows. No criminal charges were ever brought against anyone about the forged checks. Matlick was the only person whose handwriting was ever examined.

All through that confusing weekend, the phones

at the Glenview house were busy, again according to telephone company records. People called to congratulate Brach because one of her horses had just won at the Hialeah racetrack in Florida. Some of these calls were unanswered.

A call from a friend named Belton Mouras was also unanswered. Mouras was the chief executive of the Animal Protective Institute, a California charity Helen Brach supported. Mouras knew of Brach's love of animals, and he was anticipating her annual $100,000 donation. But Mouras didn't reach Helen Brach that night. He never spoke with her again.

Other callers were luckier. Matlick answered their calls. He did not, however, let anyone talk with Helen Brach. He said she had just stepped out, was in the bathtub, was indisposed, or simply unable to come to the phone at the moment.

When Richard Bailey called Brach late Sunday night, Matlick told him she'd gone out on a date. Matlick said he was surprised to hear from Bailey because he thought Brach's date was with Bailey himself. Matlick later told police Brach had gone out with a "mystery man" that evening, but that she had returned home by midnight. The identity of the mystery man remains unknown. It is also not certain whether Helen Brach had actually gone out at all.

Not every call that weekend was from someone phoning Brach. Calls also went out *from* the house. Matlick called his wife before he met Brach at the airport. He called five different branches of the

Marshall Field's department store chain. Sunday night he called to make an appointment with a cleaning and decorating service. He wanted them to come as soon as possible to repaint two rooms and replace a rug. They promised to send people out on Tuesday.

Someone in the Glenview mansion that weekend called Frank Brach's one-time physician. Whoever called reached the doctor's answering service. Helen Brach hadn't been in touch with this doctor since her husband died seven years earlier. And someone also called the Brachs' accountant, Everett Moore, at his office. That call reached his answering machine. Helen Brach knew he was never in his office on weekends.

The next morning was Monday, a freezing cold day. Matlick said he drove Mrs. Brach to O'Hare at 7:00 A.M. so she could catch her flight to Florida. That would have put Brach at the airport three hours before the earliest scheduled flight to Florida.

There were other oddities in Matlick's story of that morning. Although Brach often traveled with as many as forty pieces of luggage, on this trip Matlick reported she had carried only a small tan overnight bag. She didn't take the trunk Matlick said she had been packing when she injured her hand. Matlick said that the last time he saw her, she was wearing a black suit, a white blouse with a black bow tie, and black patent leather shoes and purse. No coat on that frigid day. No bandage on her injured hand. He also said she was carrying

$700 in cash, which she had earlier asked him to get for her. Usually she carried very little cash.

Her final words to him that morning, Matlick said, were that she would call him in ten days about sending all the other clothing she had packed.

With that, all reports of Helen Brach's whereabouts end.

None of the airlines were able to produce any evidence showing that Helen Brach had taken a plane to Florida. Police wondered why Matlick had driven Brach to the airport hours before any scheduled flight to that destination. They also wondered why Helen Brach would go to the airport without a reservation.

Jack Matlick didn't clear up these questions. Furthermore, during the next two weeks, he behaved in other peculiar ways.

After he dropped Brach off at O'Hare on Monday, he went straight back to the mansion. There, he gathered some of her jewelry and took it to a lockbox in the Glenview State Bank. The bank opened at 9:00 A.M.; Matlick arrived there at 9:05, still driving the car in which he'd taken Brach to the airport. The jewelry was later found intact.

From the bank, Matlick drove to a Cadillac dealership, where he had the car waxed and its upholstery shampooed. Workers there later told the police there had been no visible reason for the clean-up. Decorators who came to repaint rooms at the Glenview mansion on Tuesday morning said the same thing.

During the second week of Brach's absence,

Matlick hired a cook-housekeeper, which was unusual. He fed and exercised Brach's three dogs, which was expected. He waited to hear from Mrs. Brach about sending along her clothes.

When he hadn't heard anything by March 4, 1977, Matlick went to the Glenview police to file a missing persons report. He couldn't do that, police said; the next of kin had to.

So Matlick went back to the mansion and called Helen's brother, who lived in Ohio. Five days later, Brach's brother arrived. The two men burned some of Brach's diaries. Only then did Brach's brother go to the police to file the missing persons report. It was March 9, 1977.

Glenview police began their hunt for Helen Brach. They went to the mansion and found in the furnace the pile of ashes and metal binders from the diaries. Brach's brother told them he'd been following his sister's instructions when he burned the papers. He said he'd found a note from her on top of the diaries: "Burn these in case something happens to me." He said he'd burned the note, too, although he wasn't sure what he thought might have happened to Brach.

Police studied the surrounding grounds of the mansion, which had been hard-frozen for at least forty-two days. That would have made it difficult to bury any evidence of foul play. They found a newspaper clipping about urban crime dated February 2 lying on top of a pile in a desk tray. The headline was, "Will We Always Live in Fear?" Several days later, they looked at the new locks

Matlick had installed on three doors in the Glenview house — one to Brach's bedroom, one to her study, and one to her closet.

Matlick was cooperative, but he seemed frightened of something or someone. Glenview police grew suspicious of his role in Brach's disappearance.

When the Cook County Sheriff's Office offered lie detector test facilities to them, the Glenview police accepted the offer. Feeling pressured by police and the newspapers, Matlick volunteered to take the polygraph tests. For the record, Glenview police decided the results were inconclusive. Off the record, Matlick's attorney told one reporter that Matlick had failed not one but two tests.

If that's true, what was Matlick covering up?

His reports of meeting Helen Brach at O'Hare on Thursday and driving her back there the next Monday hadn't been supported by any other witnesses. Police had only his word to go on, and his word was confusing.

His version of the events of Helen Brach's last weekend in her Glenview house kept changing. His story about the injury to Brach's hand was one example of this. Another example was his story about Brach's will. First Matlick said that he'd read it and that he knew where it was. He swore under oath he knew he wasn't mentioned in it. Later he said he didn't know where the will was.

The whereabouts and contents of the will began to play an important part in the search for Helen Brach. It might give a clue to her whereabouts. It might show who stood to gain by her death.

Thirteen months after Brach vanished, a Cook County investigation conducted a search of the Glenview mansion. The date was April 1 — April Fools' Day. The search had been kept a secret. Only people who had a legal reason to be there were invited to attend.

Even more strange things surfaced then.

One of the attorneys involved in the case called the search an "Easter Egg Hunt" because objects appeared that seemed to have been planted. One of the planted objects was the missing will. It *did* mention Matlick, contrary to his original statement. But the amount Helen Brach had left him seemed too small to be a cause for foul play.

Matlick's story of that final weekend was obviously less and less truthful.

If it was only a story, then had Helen Brach disappeared right after she left the bath shop in Rochester?

Had Matlick grown so concerned about the possibility of losing his job that he went to meet Brach in Rochester? Had he become so upset that he somehow did away with her before he returned — alone — to the Glenview home? Had he helped other people somehow do away with her between Minnesota and Illinois? Could those other people have worked alone and now be threatening him, telling him to come up with a good story — or else?

As time went on with no trace of Helen Brach surfacing, many people assumed that she was dead. The most telling clue was that not once had she phoned to ask about her three beloved dogs, a highly suspicious silence.

At first when the authorities had cast about for people who would have benefited by Helen Brach's death, they saw Jack Matlick. Then their gaze fell on Belton Mouras of the Animal Protective Institute.

When the news of Brach's disappearance broke in the newspapers on March 22, 1977, Mouras was quick to hire Ernie Rizzo to search for her. Rizzo was an ex-cop turned private investigator. He was happy to accept the $1,000 a day he said Mouras would pay him to find Brach.

Rizzo and the other investigators sifted through the sightings that came in after Brach's disappearance hit the news. None of the leads panned out. Rizzo knew the Glenview police were conducting the search on their home turf; he himself would take other, different, tacks.

First, he flew to Ft. Lauderdale. Inside the Brach condominium there, Rizzo found the packages from the bath shop in Rochester. He wasted no time in flying to Minnesota to find the salesclerk. By the time he returned to Chicago, Rizzo was sure Brach had flown back from Rochester on schedule and that, once home, she had never left Glenview alive.

Later Rizzo took another approach. He talked with the Florida friends Brach had phoned before she called Matlick on her last day in Rochester. He discovered that Brach had asked them if they would go with her to a plastic surgeon in Rio de

Janeiro. She was considering getting a facelift, but she didn't want to go to a foreign country alone.

When this story broke in the papers, reporters got in touch with the plastic surgeon's secretary. She said Helen Brach hadn't checked in and didn't even have an appointment. Furthermore, Glenview police knew that her passport was still in the Glenview mansion. They'd seen it there during one of their searches. Helen Brach would not be found in Rio.

Now Rizzo, following another course, grew more and more convinced that Helen Brach's whereabouts could be traced through Jack Matlick. He investigated all the phone calls made from the Glenview house on Brach's last weekend there. He learned that Matlick had bought a meat grinder attachment for Brach's blender at a Marshall Field store. He heard that her three dogs were fed ground meat. He knew that the ground was hard-frozen when Brach disappeared. If she had met with foul play, how could her body have been disposed of?

Rizzo put two and two together and came up with the "meat-grinder theory." Had Matlick, upset over losing his job, killed Brach and disposed of her body by grinding it up and giving it to her three dogs?

This was Rizzo's final tack, and police found it outrageous. For one thing, Brach's three pets weren't big dogs. It would have taken a relatively long time for them to eat Helen Brach's 160-pound body, let alone gnaw the bones to sawdust. And that was assuming that a meat-grinding attachment for a blender could have done the job to begin with. No, Glenview police said; the meat-grinder theory wasn't a good one.

But they, too, had their suspicions about Matlick. Those suspicions were diverted momentarily on April 14, 1978, to Helen's horse trader friend, Richard Bailey. Someone had spray-painted two messages near the Brach house in Glenview. One of the messages said, "Richard Bailey knows where Mrs. Brach's body is. Stop him! Please!" The other said, "Bailey killed Brach."

Bailey told police the same messages had been painted on the stables he owned, but that he'd painted them over because he thought it might be bad for business.

In spite of the messages, it wasn't until the next year that Bailey was called to make a statement under oath. In addition to selling Brach her race-horses, Bailey had links to the Jayne family, a group of show-horse owners. He gave his statement in June 1979.

Bailey didn't say much. In fact, he didn't say anything. He refused to answer a single question, instead taking the Fifth Amendment, which allows people not to answer a question if answering would tend to incriminate them. Bailey even "took the Fifth" in response to a question about his address!

It looked as if Richard Bailey had something to hide, and his connection with the Jayne family probably had something to do with it. In March 1981, Helen Brach's brother petitioned the court to allow a reward fund to follow up on the "horse connection."

This reward was for a quarter of a million dollars, and it was the third reward fund that had been allowed by the court. None of them had turned up any leads. All of them were paid for with Helen Brach's own money.

That money was still pouring into Brach's estate. In 1981, the fourth year of her absence, the estate earned almost four million dollars. But it spent more than that on operating expenses. Brach was still missing; she was not legally dead. Her wishes still had to be fulfilled.

However, by now, nearly everyone believed Brach was dead. Most people had a good idea about how she'd died, too. One of the attorneys who had worked on the case for a long time said she had been the victim of hired killers.

Who could have hired them, and why?

Bailey and his friend Silas Jayne, perhaps, said the attorney. Silas Jayne had, after all, been convicted of conspiracy to murder his own brother George.

Richard Bailey's record was no cleaner than that of his friend Jayne. He had been sued by another rich widow for $365,000 because she felt he had duped her in a horse deal.

These were not pleasant people, the attorney pointed out, and once Helen Brach discovered they were cheating her, she refused to be conned any longer. To stop her, he claimed, the horse traders murdered her on her trip back to Glenview.

How had the murder been committed? Where was Brach's body now?

The attorney didn't know.

A few days before the fourth anniversary of Brach's disappearance, the police got what appeared to be a major break in the case. It seemed to tie in with the "horse trader theory." A convict in a Mississippi prison, Morris Ferguson, claimed he'd been offered $10,000 to pick up the body of the "candy lady" in a suburb of Rochester and rebury it in Wisconsin. Ferguson had been convicted many times of petty crimes. News of him may have come to the police through Silas Jayne, who had also done prison time.

Ferguson's story sounded fishy to police. He said he moved the body for $10,000. But at the time, there was a $250,000 reward for information leading to the discovery of the body!

Police went forward with a digging even though Helen Brach's trail had grown very cold by now. Few other clues were coming to light.

But Helen Brach's body was not found in Wisconsin.

Had the horse traders become so angry with Helen Brach that they found a way to kill her and dispose of her body so that it would never be found?

The only problem with this theory is that the horse traders were better off keeping Brach alive. She was the goose with the golden eggs. Also, most of the rumors about their having done away with her seemed to originate with the horse traders themselves.

What happened to Helen Brach?

No one knows.

Did Jack Matlick do away with her, somehow pulling off a "perfect crime"? Nothing was ever proven. Glenview police continue to "know how to get in touch with him," although he moved to Pennsylvania and continues to live there alone.

Did Richard Bailey and the Jaynes connive with Matlick to murder Helen Brach? Once again, nothing was ever proven.

Even more intriguing is the question of who cared about what happened to Helen Brach besides the attorneys and bankers and accountants who made hefty fees throughout the case.

Helen Brach had few friends and, in fact, had made some enemies as she fought for the rights of animals. Did some of her enemies — people who ran animal shelters cruelly and for their own gain — decide to get Helen Brach out of the way?

In her will, Helen Brach left most of her money to her own nonprofit foundation to aid animals. She had also planned to be buried beneath the granite-and-marble tomb she'd built in her hometown. She would lay near her parents, husband, and pets when she breathed her last.

But her grave is still empty; her body has never been found.

Helen Brach was declared legally dead on February 21, 1984 — seven years after she disappeared.

The Pirates of Cocos Island

"It looks like an open grave!" one visitor said the first time he saw Cocos Island.

The island, a small dot of jungle in the Pacific Ocean five hundred miles southwest of the Panama Canal, *is* in many ways an open grave. Many visitors to it have found weathered human bones — and all because Cocos was a perfect pirate treasure dump.

Why was Cocos perfect for pirates? For one thing, it's isolated. No other islands neighbor it out there in the vast ocean.

It's also secure. A roaring surf breaks on the rocks hemming it, leaving only one safe spot for ships to land. A small harbor lies at the island's northeast end. There, a freshwater brook runs, making the landing even more attractive to sailing ships of long ago. They could take on vital drinking water.

There are still other features of Cocos that were attractive to pirates. The land rises high and rocky in the island's center, where there are caves that were used for the storage of loot. Waterfalls that are refreshing and cool in the midst of sweltering heat spill over ledges. Plenty of coconut trees grow, which provided fresh food in place of the ships' stores of rat-nibbled, spoiled rations.

The island's terrain offered plenty of landmarks for pirates. They could bury treasure there and map its location. After all, what good is burying loot if you can't find it again?

In fact, Cocos Island was such a perfect treasure dump that at least three famous pirate captains hid fabulous booty there. Then all three vanished — along with their treasure!

The first to arrive was Edward Davis, sometime in the late 1600s or early 1700s. Before he stumbled upon Cocos Island, Davis had gained a reputation for violence at the same time that he amassed his fortune. From his home base on the island of Jamaica in the Atlantic, Davis preyed on heavily laden Spanish treasure ships as they ferried home the spoils they'd plundered from South America.

Spanish warships sought to guard the treasure ships from the swarms of pirates, privateers, and buccaneers in the Atlantic. Sometimes they chased a pirate ship all the way down one South American coastline and up the opposite one, until the outlaw ship had been safely run into the Pacific. That left the New World-to-Europe sea lanes with at least one less pirate ship for a time.

That may have been what led Davis to the Pacific

and Cocos Island. When he left the place, it was richer by 700 bars of gold, 20 water kegs full of gold doubloons, and more than 100 tons of Spanish silver coins.

According to one story, Davis and his crew sailed from Cocos straight into oblivion, never returning to reclaim their booty.

But another story says Davis sailed to Jamaica, where he retired and lived out the rest of his life peacefully.

What really happened to Davis?

That question has never been answered.

Pirates were notorious for many reasons, and one of them was never letting people know where they were or what they were doing. They liked to stage surprise strikes on their prey.

It is known that Davis had "retired" once, before he ever came to Cocos. In 1688, he left the life of a high-seas spoiler and settled down in Port Comfort, Virginia. Unfortunately, he and two of his men were recognized and arrested there. Their booty was confiscated by the king's officers, and the three pirates spent a year in the Jamestown jail.

When they were freed under a royal pardon, Davis had been as interested in getting his loot back as he was in gaining his freedom. He wanted the king's officers to return what they had confiscated. He claimed they had taken it illegally. Davis made a complete list of everything he'd lost to make *sure* he got it all back. The list included 5 bags of coins, 142 pounds of silverplate, and "fower paire of silke stocking."

After due consideration, officials said Davis could have his treasure back if he gave £300 to the founding of the College of William and Mary. Davis agreed to do that, thereby contributing to higher education in the American colonies. Officials followed through on their part of the bargain. They returned everything they'd "stolen" from Davis, right down to the four pairs of silk stockings.

When Davis left Virginia, he returned to a pirate's life. So it may be that both stories about what happened to him are correct. He may have "retired" again on Jamaica, only to become a pirate again. And it may be that he buried his loot in Cocos Island, only to vanish completely afterward.

Not all pirates were blood-and-guts types. Davis, for example, appears to have been a privateer, a state-approved pirate. Privateers were in the pirating business for the adventure of it and also for the benefit of their king or queen.

That wasn't the case with Benito Bonito, the second pirate who buried a treasure trove in Cocos Island. Bonito was in business for himself, a throwback to the old-time buccaneers. To him, keelhauling people or making them walk the plank was all part of a good day's work. He wore a sword on his hip, he hurled insults at his crew, and he laughed as he tortured his victims.

From the time he was a boy, Bonito had heard about Cocos Island. Already the place had become legendary. It was only natural that, as his career progressed, Bonito would take advantage of all the attributes that Cocos Island had to offer.

In 1814, Bonito was the captain of a Spanish privateer sailing the Atlantic. He went into business for himself after he became master of a Portuguese trading brig. He soon quarreled with the captain, settling the quarrel by murdering the captain in 1816. Bonito seized the brig and turned pirate.

His first captured prey was an English ship, which he renamed the *Relampago*, Spanish for "lightning flash." He made all the captured crew except two men walk the plank. These two saved themselves by joining Bonito's company. Bonito amassed an immense treasure from ships taken on the Atlantic. He buried all this loot on an island in the French West Indies.

Bonito's successes soon made him infamous. Warships started tracking him. To escape, Bonito sailed down the coast of South America, rounded Cape Horn, and started working the Pacific Ocean. He buried all the booty he gained during this period in Cocos.

Then Bonito sailed south again to capture a Spanish galleon that was carrying the payroll for the Spanish armies fighting in Peru. When he captured it, a Spanish warship was sent after him. Bonito ran from it, sailing north. He landed at Acapulco port in Mexico. He went ashore there, disguised as a muleteer, a driver of a mule team. He intended to get information that would help him sack the place before he moved on.

But once ashore, Bonito heard news so interesting to him that he changed his plans. He learned that a rich treasure of gold was being removed from Mexico City. Bonito returned to his ship and plotted.

That night, Bonito and part of his crew went ashore to lay in wait for the mule train carrying the gold shipment. They captured the gold train's escort troops, killing any soldier who wouldn't join them. Then the pirates redirected the treasure train to the coast. They took $11 million of treasure into the hold of their ship, and from there sailed to Cocos, where they buried it.

The island was starting to feel like home to Bonito. Then he told his crew they would be returning to the treasure cache they'd left in the West Indies. They would dig it up and ship it back to be buried in Cocos, too. His men didn't like the idea. There were too many warships in the Atlantic, they were too well known, and they'd certainly be caught.

Bonito smelled mutiny. He drew the cavalry sword at his waist and struck down the leader of the mutiny. He also killed anyone else who dared to disagree with him. The battle lasted until the next morning.

The sun rose on fifteen dead bodies littering the beach of Cocos Island. Others had been taken by the sharks. But Bonito had subdued the mutiny. His pirate ship sailed south, again rounding the Horn and heading up the Atlantic coast of South America.

For a year, Bonito's company terrorized the Brazilian coast. Finally, in 1821, a British warship cornered the pirates in the West Indies, and a desperate fight followed. By the time it was over, Bonito was finished. Some say he died during the battle, either by committing suicide or in action on his own quarterdeck.

Other accounts say he made his way back to Costa Rica alone, only to vanish mysteriously from there while attempting to raise an expedition that would take him back to Cocos Island and reunite him with his booty.

What did happen to Benito Bonito, the last of the old-time buccaneers?

No one really knows.

All the time Bonito was terrorizing the waters on both sides of South America, political conditions in Peru were being set up for the third great treasure believed to have found its way to Cocos Island.

This was known as the Lima Treasure. It would be buried by a captain of a merchant ship and its crew who had been overcome by greed. This captain's fate would also be mysterious and confusing. It was, in fact, even more so than the fates of Davis and Bonito.

It all started when Simon Bolívar began marching to Lima with the intent of liberating Peru from European rule. City and church officials and the wealthy people of Peru heard Bolívar was coming. They scrambled to save their riches from the revolutionaries.

Theirs was considerable wealth — about $30 million worth of bullion, silver and gold plate, jewels, and church ornaments, which included a life-sized, diamond-encrusted, solid-gold statue of the Virgin Mary. All of it was sent to the Spanish fort of Lima for protection.

The siege against the fort was raised in 1820. The Spanish commander directed his men to take the treasure away for safekeeping. It was loaded onto merchant ships as freight. Captains of the merchant ships promised to ferry the treasure-freight to Panama.

Captain Charles Thompson of the brig *Mary Dear* happened to be in the area. He was looking for freight after having delivered a load of coal. Some of the Lima Treasure was put on his ship, where it was placed under the protection of the British flag.

But Thompson and his crew were less than trustworthy. According to one report, Thompson said he and his men were "tempted by the glittering millions, and in the night we cut our cables and put out to sea." The Spanish chased them, but Thompson's ship was swift. It eluded capture. However, there was still the problem of hiding the loot: "We were puzzled to know what to do with the treasure," Thompson wrote in one version of his confession. "But after a consultation, decided to bury it in Cocos Island."

They sailed there and took ten or eleven landing boatloads of the Lima Treasure through the pounding surf. They buried each boatload in the island. Thompson drew a chart, then he and his crew sailed off — and vanished. One report said their ship was sunk by Spanish pirates; another, that it went down in a hurricane.

The story of the Lima Treasure is thus far a sad tale of greed. The story stayed that way for around twenty years. Then it grew mysterious — because Captain Thompson returned!

Reports of his reappearance were oddly different. He returned in a number of different places and in a number of different ways. And he died a different death in a different place in each story. But some parts of the reports were in agreement. Thompson always returned with his Cocos map — and a wish to reclaim the Lima Treasure.

One version of Captain Thompson's fate came from a whaleman from Cape Breton, Nova Scotia. This man said he'd heard Thompson's deathbed story sometime around 1842. He said Thompson told him that after he and his men buried the Lima Treasure in Cocos Island, their ship had been captured by a Spanish warship. All the company had been tried for piracy and sentenced to death. Thompson and two of the crew were spared because they promised to tell where the treasure was hidden.

This version then splits into at least three different endings. Ending number 1 has Thompson and one man being taken back to Cocos, where they landed under an armed guard. They managed to escape their captors, hiding in caves on the island. For four days armed parties looked for them, but finally the warship sailed away.

Thompson and his fellow pirate lived on wild berries and birds' eggs until a ship stopped to get fresh water. This ship took them off the island. Thompson landed on the mainland and worked his way back to England. The other pirate died of fever.

Ending number 2 again has three pirates saving their lives by promising to tell their captors where the treasure was buried. But now they said they'd buried it in the Galapagos Islands. On the voyage there to reclaim it, the Spanish ship anchored in a place where all the crew and one of Thompson's companions died of yellow fever. A whaler anchored nearby. When it sailed one night, Thompson and his remaining companion jumped ship, swam to the whaler, and were taken aboard. They were on the whaler several years, saying nothing of the treasure all that time before the ship sailed home to Nova Scotia. Once there, Thompson handed over a chart and full directions for recovering the Lima Treasure to the Cape Breton man. Then he died peacefully in bed.

Ending number 3 has a shark gobbling up Thompson's sole companion as the two swam to the whaler. Thompson, a hunted man, was taken to Jamaica. There he boarded a Newfoundland sugar vessel whose carpenter, John Keating, persuaded his unwilling captain to let Thompson remain on board. Thompson handed a chart to Keating, who smuggled him onto yet another ship, this one bound for London. Years later, Keating received a letter dictated by Thompson on his deathbed in a London hospital. The letter gave Keating full instructions on recovering the Lima Treasure.

The confusion over Thompson's true fate doesn't end there!

A completely different version of it has Thompson meeting Keating, this time on a brig bound for Newfoundland in 1844. Thompson was a stranger, a handsome passenger, and Keating was a shrewd but ignorant seaman employed on the vessel. Back in Newfoundland, Thompson told Keating the secret of the treasure cache on Cocos. Keating, in return, found a local merchant to back an expedition to reclaim it. The merchant fitted out a ship under the command of a Captain Bogue.

During all this, a lady had been listening to the handsome Thompson's yarns. She had grown fascinated by him. On a cold winter's night before the ship sailed, she dashed into the cottage where Thompson and Keating were sitting. She cried, "Fly, fly for your life. You are to be arrested immediately. Men are even now on your track! I do not know what you may have done or what crimes you are guilty of."

Thompson turned white, handed Keating a worn and soiled chart, gave him verbal directions to help him find the Cocos treasure cave, waved farewell, and dashed out the door. He was later found dead in the snow.

What all the stories share is that Thompson was the only survivor of the missing *Mary Dear* and that he had hung onto his treasure map.

By 1844, all the Thompson stories had ended. Now the mystery shifted to Bogue and Keating. In fact, the two Newfoundlanders went to Cocos armed with a version of Thompson's directions:

"Turn north, and walk to a stream. You will now see a rock with a smooth face rising sheer like a cliff. At the height of a man's shoulder from the ground, you will see a hole large enough to allow you to insert your thumb. Then thrust an iron bar into the cavity and you will find behind the door, opening outwards, the treasure."

Following these instructions, Bogue and Keating found the Lima Treasure. And what a treasure! Bars of gold; sacks of silver bearing the stamp of a Lima bank, one burst sack spilling out a silver stream of coins; the golden Madonna, too heavy for the two men to lift.

Meanwhile, back on their ship, mutiny had broken out.

Bogue, the story goes, dashed to the landing boat in an attempt to get back to the ship and put down the mutiny. But his pockets were so loaded with treasure that he drowned in the surf. Keating survived by hanging onto the floating boat. He was picked up by a passing ship and returned to Newfoundland. The mutineers had long since sailed back to Newfoundland and were spreading reports of Bogue's death that made Keating look as untrustworthy as Thompson had been.

Keating was never able to mount another expedition to find the Lima Treasure, although he tried. After his death, his wife did get an expedition together to go to Cocos Island. It returned empty-handed.

Mysteries pile on mysteries in the case of the Lima Treasure. What really happened to Bogue? What really happened to Thompson? What really happened to the treasure?

Perhaps all the variations on the Lima Treasure story simply point to the befuddlement caused by greed that rises in many people when they hear of a glorious treasure trove and dream of finding it.

Certainly the lure of treasure in Cocos Island drew wave after wave of hopeful seekers. Then, in 1935, the government of Costa Rica, which owns the island, outlawed the practice of treasure hunting. In 1978, Cocos Island became a park.

A tree trunk brought to the Costa Rica Museum from Cocos is carved with the words, "The bird is flown!" Many of the great rocks and boulders on the island bear the same inscription, put there by long-dead seafarers of all kinds. Most people take these words to mean that no treasure remains on this treasure island.

One treasure hunter lived on the island for seventeen years. He discovered only thirty-three gold coins in all this time. Finally even he gave up and moved to New York City.

The true history of Cocos Island is shrouded in half-fact and legend, as murky as the histories of those who landed there. What happened to the booty, as well as to the pirates who buried it there, also remains a mystery.

Vanished in the Bermuda Triangle

In 1948, internationally known jockey Albert Snider was riding high. He had an excellent mount, the big bay stallion Citation, from famed Calumet Farms.

He and Citation were racking up impressive victories at the Hialeah racetrack in Florida. They won the Everglades Handicap by a length. The next week, they won the Flamingo Stakes by *six* lengths. As fast as Citation ran, and as well as Al Snider rode him, the rumors around the track flew even faster.

Citation, it was said, was almost a sure bet to win the fabled Kentucky Derby. He might go even further. He could win the Triple Crown!

That distinction still belonged to Assault, the horse that had won all three races that make up the Triple Crown — the Kentucky Derby, the Preakness Stakes, and the Belmont Stakes. The Triple Crown comes to few horses and few jockeys. Winning it brings enormous rewards. Prestige is part of the Triple Crown, too — as well as money.

Al Snider wanted to be one of the jockeys to ride a horse to Triple Crown victory, and he wanted that horse to be Citation. And he was on the way to achieving his goal with those Hialeah victories. They had gotten him to the starting gate, but the race for the Triple Crown was still to be run. Derby Day would be the first real step for both him and his mount.

Snider felt that a few days at sea would help him relax to meet the challenge. He and some friends chartered a yacht for a fishing trip along the Florida Keys.

But Snider's plans went awry.

True, when Derby Day was over, Citation was victorious.

Citation was also victorious in the Belmont Stakes and the Preakness Stakes that year, becoming the second horse from Calumet Farms to wear the Triple Crown.

But Citation won that crown without Al Snider up. It was legendary jockey Eddie Arcaro who rode that great horse to those victories.

The substitution had been necessary because on March 6, 1948, six days after he and Citation had won the Flamingo Stakes, Snider and his friends vanished in the infamous Bermuda Triangle.

The waters in that treacherous area of the Atlantic swallowed them up so completely that no trace of any of them was ever found. The fishing trip Al Snider had taken to find relaxation had brought him to oblivion instead.

* * *

When he vanished in the Bermuda Triangle, Al Snider joined the ranks of a large group of people lost in this area — so many that writer John Wallace Spencer called the area the "limbo of the lost." He wrote, "Tragedies connected to this region continually occur without explanation, without pattern, without warning, and without reason."

Were Snider and his friends just a few more victims of some strange malignancy in this area? Or had they merely gotten caught in bad weather that they and their boat couldn't handle?

The answer to those questions can best be found by investigating what is known about the Bermuda Triangle itself.

Many people experienced in sailing or flying in the area say the Triangle is no more dangerous than any other area. It got its reputation as a "killer spot" only because so many of the tales that seem to indicate it's a dangerous area can't be *disproved*.

Still, even a partial list of the most famous disappearances in the Bermuda Triangle indicate something mysterious is going on there:

In 1880, the *Atalanta*, a British ship with a crew of 290 cadets, disappeared completely.

The next year, the *Ellen Austin*, another British ship, was found abandoned. It was filled with precious cargo and seaworthy, but the entire crew had vanished.

The roll call of vanished ships or crews goes on, steadily ticking off disasters:

In 1909 the *Spray*, a yacht sailed alone by Joshua Slocum, was lost. Slocum had become famous in

1898 after he'd sailed around the world by himself.

In 1918, the U.S.S. *Cyclops*, a Navy ship, disappeared.

In fact, ships of all kinds, from yacht to freighter to schooner to cargo ship, have gone missing in the Bermuda Triangle. One that disappeared in 1926 was the *Suduffco*, a freighter that some thought had been swallowed by a sea monster. In 1944, the crew of the *Rubicon*, a cargo ship, vanished. The only living creature left on board was a dog.

The strange disappearances of ships reach into the near-present time:

In 1963, *Sno'Boy*, a fishing boat that was sixty-three feet long and had forty people aboard, disappeared.

In 1967, the *Witchcraft*, a cabin cruiser, disappeared only a mile from Miami.

In 1973, the *Norse Varient* and *Anita*, sister ships both carrying coal, disappeared. They are said to be the largest cargo ships ever to vanish in the Triangle.

Not only ships come to destruction in this strange watery graveyard. Airplanes vanish, too — sometimes whole flights of them.

In 1945, for example, Flight 19, with five U.S. Navy torpedo bombers, left the Fort Lauderdale, Florida, airport and vanished. The routine training mission was manned by five pilots, five radio operators, and four gunners. One of the gunners remained behind. He'd had a strange feeling about the flight, and he had completed his required flight time for that month. So when he asked to be excused, permission was readily granted.

The flight was airborne at 2:00 P.M. Two hours later, its commander reported that his compasses were acting up. Soon after that, he radioed that "Everything is wrong . . . strange . . . even the ocean doesn't look right." He sounded confused and upset.

When the radio went dead, two seaplanes were sent to search for Flight 19. Only one returned, several hours later. The next day's extensive air-sea searches found no trace of any of the planes in Flight 19 or of the missing rescue plane.

Other victims of the Bermuda Triangle include small planes like the Piper Comanche that vanished in 1970. In fact, since the 1970s the mysterious disappearances have continued at the rate of fifty to sixty per year, according to writer Charles Berlitz. What's even more astonishing is that these disappearances, like those of Al Snider and his friends, leave behind no trace. Telltale parts of boats or planes never surface. Bodies of people who vanish never wash up anywhere.

Even the U.S. Coast Guard doesn't completely deny the reality of what many people call the "myth" of the Bermuda Triangle. One of their fact sheets says, "Extensive but futile Coast Guard searches . . . have lent credence to popular belief in the mysterious and supernatural qualities of the 'Bermuda Triangle.' "

Still, many scientists say that if all the facts were known, each loss could be explained by natural events, human error, mechanical failure, or a combination of all three.

The problem is that so few facts *are* known. This has led to a large number of intriguing theories about what happens to those lost in the area.

One theory of what might have happened to Snider and the other missing people is that they were attacked by sea monsters. This sounds funny, but in fact some very large and unknown creatures may — and probably do — live undiscovered in the ocean depths.

One was found by Danish oceanographer Anton Bruun, a scientist who maps the oceans and studies the chemistry and wildlife in them. Bruun captured an eel in 1930. The eel was a tadpole, but even at this age it was six feet long. Fully grown, the eel could be expected to measure seventy-two feet long. Whales this large are well known, and there are also reliable reports of giant squids and huge jellyfish.

Had some sort of monster appeared under Snider's fishing yacht, capsizing and smashing it?

It could have.

But Snider probably didn't disappear in that way. Most animals don't attack boats or people except in self-defense. Even if Snider or one of his fishing party had hooked a sea monster, they would undoubtedly have cut the line. Hauling in a catch bigger than your boat is a great way to sink.

Another theory of what happens to the missing in the Bermuda Triangle is that they get caught in a time warp. This sounds more like science fiction than reality. But as people have pointed out, legends become legends because they have a basis in truth. And the truth here is that something very like "a wrinkle in time" happens in the Triangle.

It happened to pilot Bruce Gernon, who was flying his small plane over the area in 1970. A cloud loomed in front of him soon after takeoff. He flew above the cloud to escape it. He couldn't. The funnel-shaped cloud closed around him. It was as if the cloud were chasing him. Some of his instruments stopped. He flew along in the cloud for a while, then managed to break free of it. The eerie flight resulted in Gernon's arriving at his destination a half-hour earlier than the normal flight time for the trip!

It was physically impossible for Gernon's plane to fly that rapidly under normal conditions. The only realistic explanation for his early arrival would have been a tail wind blowing 500 miles per hour. That strong a wind would have been noticed from the ground. None was.

So perhaps Gernon had flown into *abnormal* conditions. Perhaps that strange cloud his plane entered was a time warp — a funnel in which time is twisted out of shape.

Scientists knowledgeable in modern quantum physics are well aware that particles are unstable in time and space. The possibility that there are different time universes around us is a very real one. Albert Einstein himself theorized that time can behave differently from the way most of us expect it to. He said that time is the fourth dimension.

Another twist on the time-warp theory is the notion of time eddies. In this theory, time again takes on unexpected dimensions. Instead of always moving ahead in a straight line, it swirls. It doesn't tick off smoothly like a clock. Instead, parts of the main stream of time sometimes splinter off, like an eddy in water. Time eddies would strike like those in water, too, quickly and unexpectedly. They would carry off anything in the area with them.

Could Al Snider and others who have disappeared in the Bermuda Triangle be traveling in a time warp or eddy in a parallel universe? A place similar to our world, but in a different dimension? If so, can they escape? And if they could, what would they be like after breaking out of that other time, through that rupture in its smooth flow?

No one knows.

Readjusting how we think about time can lead to another theory of what happens to the people who are lost and never found in the Bermuda Triangle.

According to this theory, U.F.O.'s (unidentified flying objects) operated by alien beings are picking up people and/or vehicles from the Triangle. The idea here is that the aliens are capturing Earth specimens to study or to communicate with.

In his book about the Bermuda Triangle, Elwood D. Baumann wrote that more sightings of flying saucers have been reported in this area than anywhere else in the world. He describes one sighting that occurred on a forty-seven-foot fishing boat. A lot of other things were happening at about the same time as the sighting on that boat. The engine blew, and water began to fill the boat. The men on board began pumping it out.

They worked for thirty minutes, then glanced up to see two strange, bowl-like flying objects approaching. The hazy, white saucers came from a distance, picked up speed, and then . . . disappeared.

It could have been merely coincidence that these events occurred so closely together. Still, the fishermen wondered if the flying objects had caused the trouble with the boat's engine.

Had something like this happened to the yacht Snider and his friends chartered for their fishing trip?

Had some hazy saucers appeared and come at them, and instead of veering off and disappearing, taken them away somewhere? If so, where?

That final question is intriguing. People who believe in flying saucers usually think the aliens are beings from Outer Space. But if time is in fact the fourth dimension, the beings could also be from far in the future. They could be Earthlings who have learned how to handle time warps and eddies and can travel through them with ease.

Why would Earthlings from our future want to snatch Earthlings from the present?

One explanation points to a fact chilling in its implications: We today have museums showing Neanderthal and Cro-Magnon people, creatures from our own far-distant past. . . .

If time *is* the fourth dimension, people like Al Snider and his friends could have been snatched by alien beings from Earth's past, as well as from its future. Many people believe that the Age of the Neanderthals isn't the complete story of the Earth's past. These people point to advanced civilizations that once flourished here, only to vanish. The ancient Egyptians and the Mayan civilization in Central and South America are two of the examples often mentioned.

Another example is the once-glorious and powerful civilization of Atlantis. Though it is sometimes dismissed as a legend, the ancient Greek philosopher Plato wrote about the lost continent. He called it a powerful empire, where the people built temples, walls, roads, and pyramids. He said their technology was more advanced than our own today. The Atlanteans had developed powerful crystals. Unfortunately, they used them for destruction. Then, about 12,000 years ago, Atlantis sank. The whole empire vanished because of a flood or an earthquake or a cataclysmic war. Their powerful crystals sank with the empire, coming to rest on the ocean floor.

Some people think that these crystals, mentioned by Plato, may be changing gravity, magnetism, and electronic systems in the area. And that those changes may be why so many people are lost here.

Could Al Snider and the other people who've vanished in the Bermuda Triangle have been lost because of the crystals of lost Atlantis?

It's true that many of the missing people reported strange malfunctions of their equipment. These malfunctions include compasses that rotate wildly, radios that fail, and power failures of entire electrical systems. Are these due to the presence of the sunken crystals?

It's possible.

But so far neither Atlantis nor the crystals have been proven to exist.

There is one proven fact, however — one of the few established facts about the Bermuda Triangle.

That is that in the Bermuda Triangle, compasses point toward *true* north. Normally a compass points to *magnetic* north. The difference between these two is called compass variation. The variation changes as much as 20 degrees as one goes around the world.

Only in one other area does a compass point true north. That's in an area where no one has ever suspected the sinking of an ancient continent. The area is off the coast of Japan and mysterious disappearances have been reported here, too.

Normal causes may explain all the wildly spinning compasses. In the 1950s geologists discovered that the magnetic poles of our planet haven't always been steady. The poles have been reversed many times. Some electrical engineers believe that the incidents in the Bermuda Triangle may be caused by changes in our magnetic field. Those wild compasses may be the result of perfectly "normal" magnetic "storms."

Another often-reported "natural" condition in

the Triangle may have something to do with magnetic forces, too. This condition is unusual yellow hazes. These are more than fog or heavy humidity, and they are usually reported in connection with navigational instruments going dead.

Are these little-understood but completely natural forces responsible for the loss of the boat carrying Al Snider and many other planes and ships? Can confused navigational systems sink a boat? If they could, why would ships and planes be destroyed so thoroughly that no trace of them ever comes to light?

Destruction of debris may simply be a matter of our not being able to see the wreckage. It may all have sunk to the bottom, where it was swallowed up by shifting sand or quicksand. Divers have observed that the quicksands in the Bermuda Triangle can swallow up fairly large boats.

And debris on the ocean's surface can be carried off in another way, too. *Newsweek* magazine reports: "Experts point out that the swift current of the Gulf Stream quickly carries debris far from an accident site." The Gulf Stream is an especially treacherous area for boats. In it, the currents merge and form a "river" within the sea. The river races swiftly past Florida, where Snider and his friends were fishing. The Gulf Stream is large here, too — 48 miles wide and 2,100 feet long. And it's dangerous.

In fact, there are many possible explanations for the disappearances in the Bermuda Triangle. Even though this area is heavily traveled, a wary sailor or airplane pilot treats it with respect because of the number of hazards here. In addition to the little-understood magnetic effects, freak but fierce storms, strong currents, and waterspouts occur here.

Snider and his party weren't afloat during the hurricane season — the months of July, August, September, and October — so they weren't endangered by the movement of these storms through the Triangle. But lesser storms in the area can be just as violent — and they can strike without warning.

The storms are savage enough to destroy a ship. In addition to torrents of rain, the storms carry massive electrical charges. They hurl bolt after bolt of terrifying lightning. Sometimes there are reports of ball lightning as well — a rare and unexplained phenomenon. In it, a slowly moving ball of light appears. It sometimes scorches what it touches; it sometimes explodes in the air.

Could the Snider party's yacht have been sunk by a freak storm?

The Coast Guard and many others cite weather as the cause for most of the tragedies in the Triangle. Other yachts, including the forty-five-foot racing yacht *Revonoc*, have bowed to the windswept fury of a storm. Curiously, the *Revonoc* vanished off the southern coast of Florida amid what some call "wind-lashed seas" and what others say was not particularly severe weather. Many accounts of disappearances begin by noting that the skies were clear and the seas calm. Perhaps

49

this points to the occurrence of sudden storms that gather force as quickly as they depart.

Or could the Snider party have been lost to yet another natural hazard of the Triangle — the currents?

In this region of the Atlantic Ocean, winds blow constantly. Called the northeast trade winds, they are predictable. For centuries, traders have let these winds speed them on their voyages. Airflow south of the equator is known as the southwest trade winds. Together, the trade winds force water westward, creating currents. The trade winds push the water; the Earth's rotation pulls it.

Waters from the north and south meet and merge. Currents split, then join. They combine with other currents to swirl around boats. These currents can sink boats.

They can cause another hazard, too. When warm waters from the south hit the colder waters of the Atlantic Ocean, dense fog forms.

And there is still another natural danger in the area that might have caused Snider's disappearance. This danger is in the form of water eddies.

Scientists have long known that whirlpools, or eddies, occur on or near the sea's surface. These whirlpools are the same as the smaller ones to be seen in country streams. There, they pull leaves in and down. The eddies on the ocean, however, are much larger and much more frightening. They are wild, whirling currents that rush away from major ocean currents. And they can be lethal to small craft afloat on the ocean's surface.

Look at what happened in 1944 aboard a ship named the *Caicos Trader*, for example. It was towing a fishing boat, the *Wild Goose*. The two boats were over a deep part of the ocean near the Bahama Islands when the fishing boat suddenly pitched upwards. Then its nose plunged down, and the fishing boat slid into the water. It vanished completely.

The crew of the *Trader* immediately cut the tow line before whatever had sucked down the fishing boat dragged them down, too. The captain of the fishing boat, the only person aboard it, was lucky enough to swim to the surface. He was rescued, but the *Wild Goose* was gone forever.

"It looked as if it had been caught in a whirlpool," a crew member of the *Trader* said later. But there had been no sign that the two boats had been sailing through a whirlpool.

Had the *Wild Goose* been caught by a deep-sea eddy?

Were there even such things? It had long been thought that these dangerous eddies didn't occur in deep water, but only nearer to or on the surface.

Then, in 1959, a British oceanographer, Dr. John Swallow, discovered that floats he'd sunk at various depths were behaving strangely. Some floats went where they were expected to go, but others swirled off in surprising directions — and these moved ten times faster than the others. It was proof that there were indeed deep-water eddies.

When scientists from Woods Hole Oceanographic Institution studied a 300-mile circle of the ocean, they discovered an enormous variety of eddies in the Bermuda Triangle. They found no evidence that eddies were a threat to surface vessels. But that's what appears to have claimed the *Wild Goose*!

Still another natural hazard is found in the Bermuda Triangle — waterspouts. An eddy is a vortex in the water; a waterspout is a vortex in the sky. Waterspouts occur frequently in the Triangle.

When the atmospheric conditions are right, a funnel of whirling air is formed. When it touches the water's surface, it whips up spray and forms a waterspout. The spout may last no more than ten minutes. With winds traveling at 150 miles per hour, however, one doesn't take long to rip apart a boat!

Any of these natural hazards could have struck the fishing boat Al Snider and his friends chartered. The debris could have vanished by purely natural means, too.

Or still another natural phenomenon in the Bermuda Triangle could have claimed them instead. The theory in this case is a relatively new one.

According to it, there are vast pools of natural gas lying frozen under the sea in the Bermuda Triangle. Over these undersea reservoirs is a dome-like seal. When that seal is ruptured — by drilling, a quakelike movement of the Earth, a rise in temperature, or some other disturbance — an interesting chain of events can take place:

Enormous amounts of gas burst upwards. The gas molecules mix with molecules of the surrounding water. As this mixture rises to the surface, the gas breaks into smaller and smaller bubbles. This frothy, gaseous water is lighter than the surrounding water. It won't float objects — like a ship — that enter a patch of it. A ship suddenly loses buoyancy and sinks like a stone. If the gas leak is large enough, a plume of gas will rise into the air, causing engine failure in low-flying planes.

This gas-leak theory could also explain what happened to the fishing boat Al Snider was relaxing on before Derby Day.

It may also go far in explaining another unusual occurrence in the Bermuda Triangle — white water.

The airmen on Flight 19 mentioned white water — frothy, glowing light water. Christopher Columbus, who sailed these seas, wrote about it in his logs. U.S. astronauts have seen these glowing, white streaks as they looked down from space.

But what really happened to jockey Al Snider almost on the eve of riding Citation on Derby Day?

Had he and his companions fallen prey to a monster? To a deadly supernatural menace?

Or had they succumbed to a presently little-understood but completely natural phenomenon?

Or were they lost because of a combination of these with human errors and miscalculations?

No one knows for sure.

Some people won't even make guesses about it. Those who live in the area seem hesitant to talk about unusual disappearances like Al Snider's, according to writer Charles Berlitz. He says these pilots, crew, and fishermen don't speak because they fear being ridiculed or losing their credibility. Some simply feel it's bad luck to talk about the disappearances.

The question of Snider's fate will probably never be answered, any more than will be the question of what happened to the many other people and craft who have vanished in the Bermuda Triangle.

Tragic as it is, Snider's story has a bittersweet ending.

As noted earlier, following the disappearance of Snider, the owners of Citation asked Eddie Arcaro to ride the horse on Derby Day. At first unsure whether Citation was the right mount for him, Arcaro finally agreed. He rode the horse, holding him back as he and the other five Derby hopefuls left the starting gate. When he finally let his mount go, Citation smoothly passed the field to finish the race three and a half lengths ahead of the next horse.

That day, Arcaro won his fourth Derby.

And that day, too, he remembered Al Snider. He shared his winner's fee with Snider's widow. Warren Wright, who owned Citation, matched the sum.

Through those handsome gestures, Al Snider won a Derby purse that day — even though he wasn't around to ride in the race.

Dr. Bernard M. Bueche

In 1955, Bernard M. Bueche, M.D., arrived in Spotswood, New Jersey, out of the blue. Nine years later, he vanished from Spotswood as mysteriously as he had arrived.

At thirty-nine, Dr. Bueche was one of the only three general practitioners in the borough. During his medical practice there, he had built a clinic on Summerhill Road. He occupied one office and rented space to other medical professionals.

On July 14, 1964, he walked into the office of one of his tenants, a dentist, and said he'd be away for a few hours. Then Dr. Bueche got into his car and left.

Bueche had been known to vanish occasionally for a few weeks at a time, but he always returned to resume his practice. This time he didn't. The hours he mentioned to the dentist stretched into days, then years, and then — apparently — forever.

Police put out a missing persons report in the

summer of 1964 and made a thorough check into the circumstances of Dr. Bueche's disappearance. There was no evidence of foul play, and the doctor had not been charged with any crime. Soon the police could go no further in their search. The police chief did what he could. He concluded that Bueche "is just missing."

A year after he vanished, Dr. Bueche's medical degrees still hung on one wall of his office. All his medical equipment remained in place. His medical records were locked in his office. His second car, a small white Volvo, sat in the clinic parking lot, two of its tires flat.

Divorced, Dr. Bueche had lived in a room in the clinic, where he kept all his personal belongings. They were left behind, too. So was all his money.

Even his name remained in the phone book for a time. "We needed a doctor a few months ago," one Spotswooder told a local newspaper reporter after Dr. Bueche disappeared. "We looked in the phone book and called him. We told the nurse we were looking for Dr. Bueche. 'Fine,' she said, 'so are we.' "

What happened to Dr. Bueche?

The mayor of Spotswood answered this question with one of his own: "Why should anyone *care* what happened to Dr. Bueche?"

One angry patient *did* care what had happened to Bueche, but not for the usual reasons in a missing persons case. "A doctor's supposed to be ready to serve twenty-four hours a day," this patient snapped. "He hasn't been ready for seven months."

Another, more tolerant, patient also cared about what had happened to the doctor. "We always thought of him as a good doctor, even if he was a strange fellow. The only thing is, he's got my kids' records locked up in his office, and we need them for school."

No great mourning followed Dr. Bueche's disappearance. Perhaps that was because he *was* a strange fellow. He talked little, not even speaking to his patients except when it was necessary. He seemed to make no attempt to build friendships. He lived alone, and he brooded. He took long, solitary walks in the fields around town. In short, he kept to himself.

With such a great interest in privacy, why had Bueche come to Spotswood in the first place? Keeping to oneself is extremely difficult in a small town where everybody knows everybody else's business.

Still, Dr. Bueche became a leader in Spotswood, even though he was an eccentric. In addition to not talking much, he was also in the habit of wearing a coonskin cap over his flaming red hair when he took his solitary rambles through the town's surrounding fields.

Dr. Bueche's importance in Spotswood was due largely to his impressive medical practice. He was graduated from the University of Michigan medical school. He had taken his residency in New

York City. When he came to Spotswood, he rapidly became the most successful medical practitioner in town. His educational background and medical experience probably weren't as important to the townspeople as something else, though. He was willing to make house calls.

Dr. Bueche's practice grew, and he decided to build a hospital. He went to architect Robert O'Neill and said he wanted to build a twenty-room clinic.

O'Neill thought Dr. Bueche was joking. The clinic was much larger than it needed to be to serve the borough. The architect decided to humor Bueche, however, and he drew up plans for a modernistic, rambling building on "stilts" — concrete pylons. Dr. Bueche looked at the plans and was delighted with them. He accepted them immediately, forking over the money necessary to build the clinic. Reports of the cost range from $150,000 to a quarter of a million dollars.

Expensive as it was, the clinic was built by 1959, "stilts" and all. It was blue-paneled and decorated in plastic. It gave the town of Spotswood a big-city, if whimsical, identity.

Dr. Bueche moved into the clinic, recruiting two more doctors and the dentist to join him in offices there. For several years, he worked in this location.

Then he left.

Why?

Was Bueche simply a loner, one of those people

who are without friends because they choose to be? If so, why had he chosen to come to a small town?

Some people have suggested that both Dr. Bueche's appearance in Spotswood and his disappearance from it have something to do with the F.B.I.'s Protected Witness Program. In this program, those who give information do so only by placing themselves in danger. In order to protect these witnesses, they are given new identities in a new place of residence.

This explanation hardly seems likely, given red-headed Dr. Bueche's rambling walks. Anyone going around in a coonskin cap would be certain to attract attention. And building an oversized clinic on stilts would be another good way to draw attention.

Then, might Dr. Bueche's disappearance have had anything to do with that clinic building? Some people believe that is the case.

When Bueche left, he owed over $6,500 in 1963 property taxes, plus another several thousand dollars for 1964. Perhaps Dr. Bueche was simply having trouble meeting his bills. He left them behind, say these people, along with nearly everything else he owned.

Whatever caused his disappearance and wherever he went, Dr. Bueche's clinic continued to be useful. In December 1964, the borough foreclosed on the "doctor's office on stilts" to collect its debt. The building now houses the officials of Spotswood — the town offices and the police department.

What happened to Dr. Bernard M. Bueche?

No one knows.

But certainly some of the people whose house calls he answered must have been glad he was there . . . for a while.

Colonel Percy Harrison Fawcett

Intrepid explorer Colonel Percy Harrison Fawcett's last words to the world were in a dispatch dated May 29, 1925. Fawcett, his son, and a third explorer — his complete expedition — had reached camp on the edge of Brazil's nearly impenetrable high-plains Matto Grosso jungle. Fawcett wrote:

Here we are at Dead Horse Camp, the spot where my horse died in 1920. Only his white bones remain. My calculations anticipate contact with the Indians in about a week or 10 days, when we should be able to reach the waterfall so much talked about. . . . Our two guides go back from here. They are more and more nervous as we push further into the Indian country. . . . We shall not get into interesting country for another two weeks. I shall continue to prepare dispatches from time to time, in hopes of being able to get them out eventually through some friendly tribe of Indians. But I doubt if this will be possible.

Fawcett was right. No more messages ever got out.

Still, many people waited eagerly for the dispatches that never came. Fawcett's expedition was of great interest to them. Some of the interest was fueled by gold fever; some by scientific curiosity.

All those waiting for word from the colonel knew that if a message could be gotten out of the vast, forbidding Matto Grosso, Fawcett was the one who could do it. The explorer had first trekked into the Matto Grosso in 1906. He'd been sent to help the government of Bolivia chart their boundary with neighboring Brazil. He emerged from the jungle in 1909, his job completed.

Fawcett had been a good choice for that job. He had all the necessary skills and experience. He was a trained engineer in the British Army and had been stationed in Southeast Asia, in Ceylon, at the turn of the century. There, he'd spent much of his free time searching for the tombs and hidden treasure of Ceylon's ancient Kandyan Kings. He'd won a Founder's Medal from the Royal Geographical Society for his achievements in advancing geographical science. The Society is a British organization dedicated to that end.

If Fawcett knew how to survive in jungles and had had the technical knowledge to complete the boundary survey in 1906–1909, why would he vanish in the Matto Grosso twenty-four years later?

One possible explanation lies in the danger of the area. Mapping that boundary, for example, wasn't an easy job. In fact, the difficulties were so great that even today some of the area is uncharted. Jungle trails were webbed waist-high with clinging vegetation. Mosquitoes and other insects swarmed, and so did blood-sucking bats. Those who entered this jungle were faced with masses of poisonous snakes; other wild animals were equally deadly. Jungle illnesses could strike suddenly and with fatal results. The tribes that lived in the area protected their territory fiercely against both members of neighboring tribes and white men.

The difficulties were so great that it took Fawcett three years to finish the boundary survey. He emerged from the jungle in 1909 determined to return and face an even bigger challenge.

He'd heard about an ancient city to be found somewhere in the tangled wilderness. It was a ruined city, and it was packed with treasure. Even without the lure of gold, the city's artifacts were valuable. Here could be the real cradle of civilization! It was a city 5,000 years older than the first known cities of Egypt, and it was a city that Fawcett meant to find. His intent wasn't merely to add more luster to his already great fame. He was lured by the mystery of the city itself.

His route to the ancient city after 1909 was detoured. It led first to a library in Rio de Janeiro, which was then the capital of Brazil. Here, in the Biblioteca Nacional, Fawcett found Manuscript No. 512. The rare document convinced him that the ancient city truly did exist and that it was everything he wanted it to be. It was a city worthy of one of the greatest explorers of his day.

The manuscript reported that the lost city clung to the side of an unreachable cliff. It had been discovered by a native guide who had led a huge Portuguese expedition into the Matto Grosso in 1743. That expedition had been searching for the gold, silver, and diamond mines found even earlier by a soldier of fortune named Mechior Dias-Moreya.

The natives called this man Moribeca. He was said to be the discoverer of the incredible mineral wealth of central Brazil in the early seventeenth century. That there was great mineral wealth isn't in doubt. So much wealth was there, in fact, that during the eighteenth century, Brazil alone produced 44 percent of all the gold in the world.

But Moribeca, the manuscript went on, wouldn't tell the Portuguese where the mines were. The Portuguese threw him in prison, where he died in 1622. His tantalizing secret died with him.

But the Portuguese weren't ready to give up on those fabulous mines. As late as 1743, they were still mounting expeditions to find them.

Their expedition of 1743 was the important one, as far as Fawcett's dream of finding the lost city was concerned. But it hadn't turned out to be so important in terms of finding the mines for the Portuguese. They not only didn't find the mines, but they also got lost themselves.

Disoriented, not knowing where they were or

where they were going, the remnants of the expedition straggled northward through what is now the Matto Grosso, following their native guide. Somewhere in the jungle, they accidentally stumbled into a steep crevice.

The crevice could have been a death trap, but the men came upon an artificially made break in the cliff wall. They found themselves walking through the break onto ancient paved steps. Once through the cliff wall, they found something even more incredible.

Before them lay the ruins of a majestic city. Huge buildings and temples stood along wide streets. The Portuguese were astonished. They copied the buildings' and temples' mysterious inscriptions and brought them back. The inscriptions are still undeciphered. No one knows what they mean or who made them.

If the Portuguese in the wandering expedition of 1743 were amazed by the city, they were astonished by the treasure they saw there. It was all free for the taking — massive gold deposits making a nearby river glitter, precious stones abounding. It was almost too much for them to take in. And it was certainly too much for them to pack out.

The Portuguese faced other troubles, too. Their expedition was out of food and other necessary supplies. In the end, they had to abandon the city and struggle to find their way back to civilization.

Only three expedition members made it back, and it took them eleven years.

The three finally stumbled into the coastal state

of Bahia to report their find. Their "wild tale" was duly noted in the manuscript in the Rio library. Then it was forgotten.

The contents of the report were very nearly as lost as the city itself until Fawcett ferreted out the manuscript. The document fired his imagination. More importantly, it confirmed his belief that the city was actually out there, somewhere in the wild vastness of the Matto Grosso.

Fawcett named the city Z and began making plans to find it, but they were interrupted by the start of World War I. Fawcett went to serve on the Western Front. Having survived the war's poison gas and bullets, he returned to Brazil after the war.

The city Z still fed his imagination. He mounted an expedition to find it in 1920. The expedition failed. Fawcett's companions weren't up to the trek's demands. The expedition had had to turn back when they reached Dead Horse Camp, which is now called Camp Fawcett.

Fawcett managed to get the men on this expedition back to civilization, but he was bitter about their "softness." He compared the men on this ill-fated expedition with the men of the 1743 Portuguese party. He found his men lacking the fortitude of the Portuguese.

Tough and self-reliant, Fawcett decided that his next expedition would be more to his taste. He wanted to travel fast and with little equipment, to live off the land and the generosity of the few friendly Indians he would meet.

In 1924, he submitted a plan for this new expedition to the Royal Geographical Society. It would be a small one, he said, made up of only Fawcett himself, his son Jack, and another young Englishman, Raleigh Rimmel. He presented the route he proposed to take to Z. He and his two companions would travel light. He asked the Society to fund this expedition.

What? No supplies? the Society asked.

Fawcett replied that "no expedition could carry food for more than three weeks, for animal transport is impossible owing to the lack of pasture and to blood-sucking bats." (These bats, perhaps the source of the vampire legend, commonly prey on cattle and other beasts of burden.)

As for porters, Fawcett told his sponsors, "Most of the tribes fear and hate their neighbors, and Indians will rarely accompany you beyond the limits of their own territory."

But a party of so few people? the Society questioned.

Fawcett explained that food was a problem for a larger group: "Game is nowhere plentiful in this country; there is usually enough to feed a small party, but never a large one."

Fawcett had painted a less-than-pleasant picture of the reality his party would face in the jungle. Some in the Society questioned if the scientific gain of his expedition would be great enough to counter all the difficulties.

Fawcett said, "Science will, I hope, be greatly benefited, geography can scarcely fail to gain a good deal, and I am confident that we shall find the key to much lost history."

Besides that, Fawcett argued, there were only three men who knew where Z was. The last attempt of one of these men, a Frenchman, had cost him an eye. He probably wouldn't try again. The second man who knew the location of Z was an Englishman. He had left Brazil while suffering an advanced stage of cancer and was probably already dead. The third man was Fawcett himself. The scientific and mineral riches of the lost city might be lost forever if he didn't go to the ruins.

Fawcett's defense of his expedition convinced the Society. They approved his plans, saying they would fund his party for the two years Fawcett estimated it would take to complete the mission.

So Fawcett and his two companions started out.

People back home waited for news, only to receive that final dispatch from Dead Horse Camp.

The Royal Geographical Society noted Fawcett's matter-of-fact statement of the impossibility of getting any further word out until journey's end. For two years, the Society waited, granting Fawcett time. The impossible might, after all, happen, given the man's background and expertise.

When the impossible hadn't happened by 1927, a Society spokesman made an announcement. He said the Society was ready "to help any competent and well-accredited volunteer party" with a good plan to go into Brazil's interior to search for news of Fawcett. He said the volunteers would be going for news only and not to bring Fawcett back.

Producing Fawcett or any member of his party was out of the question, the Society's spokesman added, as Fawcett himself had pointed out when he proposed to go "where none but he could hope to penetrate and pass."

Thousands of adventurers heard this announcement, but they took it as an appeal to search for Fawcett. Many of those thousands of adventurers volunteered to find him, even though the Brazilian government thought Fawcett's exhausted and starving expedition had been killed by "one of the various tribes" on their route.

Still, reports that Fawcett, at least, was alive began filtering in from all over Brazil.

One man, a sergeant in the French Army, was especially inventive. As early as November of 1927 he published a report in a Rio newspaper. He and some friends had been shooting alligators in a river near the beginning of the party's route, he said. They saw an old man with long, gray hair. The old man was the right age to be Fawcett, and the sergeant had noted a soldierly air about him. The old man had been sitting exhausted by the side of the road, watching a colony of mosquitoes and other insects settle to work on his legs. The sergeant said something about the insects to the old man. The old man had replied mildly, "Those poor animals are hungry, too." The party of alligator hunters, so the newspaper report said, went on their way, "leaving the poor man calmly watching the mosquitoes devouring his legs."

The same sergeant also made some other reports. Once he said that Fawcett was living in luxury on a fine ranch in Brazil's interior.

Then again, he said he knew that Fawcett had given up on the civilized world and become a blissful jungle tramp.

Or again, that Fawcett had gone mad in the jungle and that Indians found him and made a god of him.

Then the sergeant switched gears and "discovered" the whereabouts of Fawcett's son Jack. Jack, he said, was living in Lima, Peru. He'd begged the sergeant not to tell the British government where he was because the Fawcett party had officially been declared dead. If the man told, Mrs. Fawcett would stop receiving a large pension.

Were any of this man's stories true?

Almost certainly not. In fact, Mrs. Fawcett never received a pension of any kind. The sergeant's reports were the worst kind of fiction. They served only to confuse an already muddled issue.

The question remained. What had happened to Colonel Fawcett?

Commander George Dyott's findings were less fanciful than the French sergeant's. Dyott was a fellow of the Royal Geographical Society, and he led an expedition of inquiry into the Matto Grosso in May 1928. His large, well-equipped party followed Fawcett's three-year-old trail from Dead Horse Camp.

Dyott interviewed an Indian chief, who told him that Fawcett's companions — his son Jack and Rimmel — had become physical wrecks by 1925. They were almost unable to speak. Fawcett had practically carried both men across a treacherous river into the unknown regions lying east, still intent on finding Z. The Indians of the two tribes on each side of the river had watched the campfires of the white men for five days. On the sixth, the fire went out. The three men had been killed by the members of another fierce tribe that lived on the opposite bank of the river, said the chief.

But Dyott heard a different story from the Indians on the opposite side of the river. The story there was that the first chief had himself killed the members of the Fawcett party. Dyott noted that this chief's son wore a curious metal charm on a necklace. It was a small plate with the name of a supply firm that had furnished Fawcett with airtight cases in 1924.

The metal plate could have been a gift. It could have been taken from abandoned equipment. It could have been a spoil of murder. Whatever that plate meant, Dyott was convinced it was time for him and his men to clear out of the area.

Waiting until night fell, Dyott and his party paddled away in canoes, leaving most of their supplies behind. He never found Fawcett's remains. Once home, Dyott announced that he thought Fawcett was probably dead, that hostile Indians had killed him.

That was also what the Brazilian government had concluded, but it was hard news for many people to accept.

Colonel Fawcett's popularity had made him almost a legend. He never seemed to fall prey to sickness; he never seemed to tire. Few people wanted Fawcett to be weak, to be vulnerable, to be dead. Most still wanted to know what had happened to him. They listened to what a Swiss, Stephen Rattin, who had been trapping in the heart of the Matto Grosso in 1931, had to say.

Rattin reported seeing a "tall man, advanced in years, with blue eyes and a long beard." The man wore animal skins and was living with an unknown tribe near the Fawcett party's projected route.

Rattin spoke with this man in broken English. The man identified himself as a captive and a colonel in the English Army. Oddly, he never said he was Fawcett. Instead, he asked Rattin to contact Major T. H. Page, a friend of his who lived in São Paulo. Tell him that I am alive, the white captive said to Rattin, but that my son is "asleep."

"Asleep" may have been the only way to say "dead" through the broken language barrier. And Major Page *had* helped finance Fawcett's last expedition. Further, before the Indians dragged him off, the captive flashed a signet ring that Mrs. Fawcett later identified as her husband's.

Many people were convinced that Rattin's story was authentic and that the captive white man he'd found was Fawcett.

But the expedition Rattin mounted to prove he'd found Fawcett was a failure.

Had Rattin discovered what had happened to Fawcett?

If his English had been better, his story would have been more solid. It might have answered for all time the question of what happened to Fawcett.

To be honest, if Rattin's expedition hadn't failed, the solidity of his story wouldn't have mattered. The question would still have been answered. But when both story and expedition were less than firm, the fate of Fawcett continued to be in question.

Later expeditions, sometimes three in a single year, were mounted. Sometimes the reports supported the "murdered by Indians theory" of Fawcett's disappearance. Sometimes the Indians murdered the party just because they were there. Sometimes they murdered out of mercy caused by the near-death state in which the men were found.

Even as late as 1955, there were reports of seeing an aged white man in the Matto Grosso who "could have been" Fawcett. And, surprisingly enough, even now stories continue to come from Brazil about what happened to Fawcett, the most famous of all missing explorers.

But none of the stories has revealed what happened to Fawcett and his party.

No remains of any of them have ever been found.

No more is certain about their fate in the jungle than is known about that mysterious ruined city they sought to find — the fabulous Z.

Maybe the more intriguing questions today are: What happened to Z? Could it still be hidden in the Matto Grosso?

James Riddle Hoffa

On the morning of July 30, 1975, former Teamsters Union president James Riddle Hoffa received a telephone call at his cottage on Lake Orion in Michigan. It was a call he'd been expecting.

Two hours after the call came, Hoffa got into his dark green 1974 Grand Ville Pontiac. When he did, he probably used the survival technique he'd long taught his valued aides. He was, after all, being watched. His phones had been tapped. Hidden federal agents were filming everyone who came and left either of his houses.

The way to enter a car in Hoffa's world? It was complicated, but safer: Put the right leg in, leaving the left leg out while starting the car. Even if the car was rigged to explode, there remained a fifty-fifty chance you'd survive. An explosion would blow a person out of the car. A person might lose his leg or be injured on the right side of his body, but he still had a chance to survive.

And you always locked your car when you left

it. That made it a little harder for someone to get in to booby-trap it.

Once in the car, Hoffa put on dark glasses and drove off for his meeting. Only two short weeks earlier, Hoffa had told one of the few union associates he trusted about the call. He said it would put him — finally — in position to regain control of the Teamsters. He'd always thought of the Teamsters as *his* union. It came first, before his family or friends, before even the union members themselves.

Hoffa had built the Teamsters, taking his ideas from the book *The Rise and Fall of the Roman Empire*. It had been a long process. But when he became general president of the International in 1958, it all seemed worthwhile to him. He'd moved from Detroit to Washington, D.C., and he'd continued to amass power. At one point Hoffa had had the power to paralyze the nation by calling for a strike of over-the-road truckers.

Part of his power came from sources outside his union. One of these important sources was the love Americans have for automobiles. This had resulted in the building of miles and miles of excellent interstates, while miles and miles of railway tracks crumbled. Anyone who could stop the trucks could also stop the moving of anything in America. Hoffa could stop the trucks.

He *would* stop them, too — if it suited his purpose. Hoffa and his high-level union associates were tough, violent, streetwise. Their policies were contrived equally to raising the standard of living of rank-and-file union members and to the lining of their own pockets.

Hoffa's power was threatening to others. The federal government's policies toward the Teamsters through various administrations aimed for two ends. One was placating the union in order to gain campaign contributions and votes. The other was undermining the Teamsters' power.

According to insiders, calculated deals involving the Teamsters were cut quickly under the table. Dealing in secrecy like this tends to attract others who deal in secrecy — the underworld of organized crime, for example, or the owners of businesses with an eye on profits who are looking for "sweetheart" contracts.

Loyalty was highly prized in this world, but it was seldom found. This, said insiders, was a world outside the law.

James Hoffa was a power in this world.

Then he was thrust out of it. He was convicted of jury tampering and pension-fund fraud. These were federal crimes, and Hoffa faced serving time in a federal prison. He appealed the convictions from court to ever-higher court. Finally the Supreme Court, the highest court in the nation, turned down his last appeal. The vote was close — five to four.

Chief Justice Earl Warren wrote the dissenting opinion in Hoffa's jury-tampering case. He said that the methods the Justice Department under

Robert Kennedy had used to convict Hoffa were "an affront to the quality and fairness of federal law enforcement." The Justice Department had, in effect, set Hoffa up for the conviction. Warren wrote that in doing so, the government "had reached into the jailhouse to employ a man who was himself facing indictments far more serious than the one confronting the man against whom he offered to inform."

The testimony of the government's witness may have been gained in a shoddy way, but the Supreme Court majority upheld Hoffa's conviction.

He surrendered to federal authorities in March 1967, and was transported to the federal penitentiary at Lewisburg, Pennsylvania. He had two sentences to serve, one for eight years and one for five. He would serve them consecutively. Even if he were never granted parole, he would be free again in thirteen years. Free — and able to resume his presidency of the Teamsters.

So Hoffa planned for that future. He turned over the reins of the Teamsters Union to Frank E. Fitzsimmons. Hoffa felt sure Fitzsimmons would step aside once he himself was free. He was also sure that Fitzsimmons would follow his orders while he was in prison. He thought he could continue to run the union from inside the prison gates through Fitzsimmons. He left one more order — Fitzsimmons should work for Hoffa's early parole.

But Fitzsimmons wasn't about to step aside, and

Hoffa was never paroled. Instead, he was given a presidential pardon by President Richard M. Nixon in 1971.

Hoffa was happy to be released. He signed the necessary papers. Later, he discovered he had also signed an agreement to avoid involvement in Teamsters affairs until 1980.

Insiders say Hoffa never saw that restriction. If he had, they said, he would never have accepted its terms. They say the note was added — illegally — by the Justice Department.

Still, Hoffa *did* sign those papers, and he was released. He emerged from the gates of the Lewisburg penitentiary, turning to raise a clenched fist at his fellow inmates as the network television cameras outside taped the scene . His determination to regain control of the Teamsters as soon as possible was strong.

Home again and now aware of the eight-year period for which he was legally barred from working with the Teamsters, Hoffa tried to overturn that restriction. He withdrew money hidden in the numerous sewer traps in his basement to pay attorneys. He made other payoffs as well, buying the loyalty and support of influential Teamsters. He continued to work behind the scenes, pulling strings. He also compiled a long, bitter list of enemies he would destroy once he was back in power.

And now, finally, on July 30,1975, the thing had come together!

The call had come; the meeting was set. Hoffa was sure he would be given documents that would overturn the restriction. His rise to power in the Teamsters would soon be rolling freely. And it would begin right after this meeting.

Hoffa got into his car and headed for the meeting place. It was an elegant restaurant, the Machus Red Fox, in a shopping center seven miles northwest of Detroit, at Fourteen-Mile and Telegraph Roads.

But something Hoffa didn't expect happened that day.

If Hoffa met the men who had phoned him, he didn't meet them in the Red Fox. And he didn't meet them in the parking lot of the shopping center.

Whatever really happened, by 6:00 P.M. the next day, Jimmy Hoffa was a numbered missing persons file.

Someone abducted him. His car was left behind in the parking lot, unlocked.

Because of the violence that surrounded the lives of Hoffa and his associates, there were few who doubted the upshot of what had happened to him: Whoever abducted Hoffa had also murdered him and disposed of his body.

Months passed. No trace of Hoffa showed up. His family and friends offered a $300,000 reward for information about his fate.

Government investigators and private citizens searched through landfills, woods, waterways, and garbage disposals for the missing man. But whoever snatched and executed Hoffa had been thorough and competent.

Hoffa's remains didn't turn up in those early months. They haven't turned up to this day.

What happened to Hoffa?

Investigators seeking answers to that question plunged immediately into murky waters. Their reports begin with assertions of hired killers, then take one step aside into stories of criminal conspiracies. The answers draw in both the underworld and the highest reaches of our nation's government. Each step into the quagmire of Jimmy Hoffa's disappearance was planted firmly enough, however — in dark and shadowy lawlessness, lies, and greed.

The story from one government informant was that Hoffa's body had been stuffed into a fifty-five-gallon oil drum and taken to an unknown destination. Earlier this informant and an associate of his had killed a man they'd had some trouble with in a loan-sharking scheme. They'd stuffed that body into the trunk of a tree somewhere. It had never been found, either. This man's story indicated that it was easy to "lose" a body.

Another government informant, a former underworld assassin, told government investigators that Mob leaders who had once worked with the C.I.A. had ordered Hoffa's death. Earlier the two groups — the Mob and the C.I.A. — had plotted the murder of Cuban leader Fidel Castro. That scheme hadn't succeeded. But the scheme to do away with one of the mobsters involved *had*. Sam Giancana had been killed because he'd become unpredictable, out of control. Hoffa, this man said, had had to be killed for the same reasons. Both Giancana and Hoffa might betray the secrets of the Castro assassination plot. That plot was somehow linked with the assassination of President John F. Kennedy. Leaking information about the one would leak information about the other, and that would be dangerous.

"Hoffa is now a . . . hubcap," this man said. "His body was crushed and smelted." Hoffa's body had been crushed in a steel compactor for junk cars.

And the union official Hoffa's family had raised from childhood, Chuck O'Brien, said much the same thing: "Hoffa is now just a fender, being driven around by someone."

Is that what happened to Jimmy Hoffa?

The true answer hinges on the events of July 30, 1975, the day he disappeared.

The official report of Hoffa's last day was put together by the Justice Department and the F.B.I. It goes something like this:

A little before noon on July 30, Hoffa left home, telling his wife he was going to a meeting at the Red Fox and would be home later that afternoon. His wife, according to the official report, said Hoffa was nervous about the meeting. She said he told her the names of the men he planned to meet.

One of the men, Anthony Provenzano, also known as Tony Pro, ruled an important East Coast Teamsters local. He had risen to that position through the ranks of one of the major crime families in the East. This man had been Hoffa's friend and supporter since the early days. In the mid-1960s, he'd been convicted of extortion and served almost five years in prison at the same time as Hoffa. It was reported that he and Hoffa had quarreled bitterly. After his release from prison, Tony Pro became one of the major supporters in the East of Hoffa's enemy Fitzsimmons.

The other man was a major figure in organized crime circles in Detroit. Anthony Giacalone was reported to be an "enforcer" of Mob orders. He'd been arrested fourteen times. He had been convicted only once — for bribing a police officer. Giacalone wasn't a union member, but he *was* a close friend of many Teamster leaders, including Hoffa. He was trying to set up the meeting between Hoffa and Tony Pro in order to make peace between them. The meeting was a "sitdown" to mend fences.

The official report goes on:

On his way to the meeting at the Red Fox, Hoffa stopped at the offices of a limousine service, Airport Service Lines. He asked to see the owner, Louis Linteau. Linteau was a friend of Hoffa's. At one time he'd been an officer of a Teamsters local in Pontiac, Michigan. He had lost that job after he'd been convicted of embezzlement. When Hoffa stopped, Linteau was out eating lunch.

Hoffa waited a while, chatting with Linteau's employees and telling them he was on his way to a meeting at the Red Fox. He mentioned the names of the men he was meeting and said he wanted to have Linteau go with him. When Linteau didn't return, Hoffa grew impatient. He got back into his car and drove off.

Hoffa reached the Red Fox in the early afternoon, at just about the time agreed on for the meeting, the official report says. He waited a half hour, then called Linteau, who had returned to his office. Hoffa told Linteau the men he'd planned to meet were late.

In fact, the men had no intention of showing up. One was actually in New Jersey, and the other was in a Detroit athletic club, getting a haircut.

After he talked with Linteau, Hoffa called his wife to say the men were late, but that he would wait for them. He went back to his car. At least two bystanders later said they saw Hoffa at about two in the afternoon, standing by his car in the parking lot as if he were waiting for someone.

A maroon Lincoln or Mercury drove up. Three men were inside. The car was like one owned by the son of one of the men Hoffa had planned to meet. The driver was a man who had switched allegiance when Hoffa was in prison. Their greetings seemed friendly. They talked with Hoffa briefly, then Hoffa got into the backseat of the maroon car and it drove away.

Once in the car, Hoffa was knocked unconscious. The car drove away from the shopping center and into Detroit. On the way Hoffa was either shot or strangled. His body was disposed of in an incinerator.

That's the official explanation of what happened to Jimmy Hoffa on his last day.

But there are other, unofficial reports that contradict this one.

One of the most intriguing unofficial reports comes from the same man Hoffa had told about the phone call he was expecting.

According to this man, a lot of the official explanation of Hoffa's disappearance didn't ring true. It sounded fishy to him for several reasons.

One was that Hoffa's words to his wife as he left home the day he disappeared were entirely out of character. He wouldn't have told his wife where he was going, who he was planning to meet, or when he'd be back home.

This wasn't so much a matter of keeping his wife in the dark as it was a way of protecting her. Later, if anyone broke into the house and questioned her — which was not unheard of in this world — she could honestly say she didn't know. *Perhaps* they wouldn't harm her if she didn't know anything.

The man said that being closemouthed about schedules was the way Hoffa and his associates dealt with one another, too. What you didn't know, you couldn't testify to in court. The less anyone knew, the safer you were. That secrecy extended even to unimportant meetings. The man talked about being taken to some of these meetings by Hoffa and not knowing who would be there until he got there.

It's hard to square this attitude with the notion that Hoffa would hang around Linteau's offices, chatting with the employees and telling them who he was meeting and where. That sort of thing just wasn't done.

Nor, according to this man, would Hoffa have hung around chatting for so long that he arrived at the Red Fox at the *approximate* time for the meeting. Hoffa was punctual to a fault. He might have waited fifteen minutes or so for latecomers, but then he would have climbed into his car and left. The only reason he might have waited longer than usual this time was because he was waiting for the information he believed he'd been promised in the telephone call.

This man's version also takes issue with the identities of the men federal agents said picked up Hoffa that day. The night before, he said, he'd been with the man federal agents said drove the maroon car. Not only was the alleged driver leaving the next day for Florida, but he was also concerned about his relationship with Hoffa. He wanted to repair it. He'd tried to talk with Hoffa on the phone several times. Always Hoffa had spoken abusively before he slammed down the receiver. The "driver" knew Hoffa would be violent toward him at first sight. There would have been no quiet, peaceful conversation.

And, continued this man's version, if the men in that maroon car had been people from the underworld whom Hoffa didn't know, he wouldn't have gotten into the car quietly. He would have done what he had to do in order to survive. He would have fought.

All the official speculation on whom Hoffa intended to meet that afternoon was silly, too, according to this man. Hoffa's phones were tapped. Whoever made the telephone call to his cottage at Lake Orion was speaking into the tape recording machines of federal agents at the same time they spoke to Hoffa.

No, this man said, there were too many errors in the official report. It didn't ring true. It wasn't "right."

Could Hoffa have overturned all his usual practices and habits on his last day?

Perhaps, if he had strong enough reasons for it. Certainly the documentation that could put him back into the leadership of the Teamsters was important.

But even that couldn't have caused Hoffa to change *all* his habits and practices. Federal agents said he'd left his car unlocked, for example. Locking his car was second nature to Hoffa. Such strong habits simply don't get changed easily.

Even if Hoffa *had* somehow miraculously changed all his habits and practices on his last day, this man's version of its events includes his own eyewitness account of them. And what he saw casts severe doubt on the official report.

The man said he'd stopped at the Red Fox shopping center that noon while on the way to a meeting of his own in Flint. He had spotted Hoffa walking around his car with his usual bantam-roosterlike attitude. He hadn't wanted Hoffa to spot him, because Hoffa might have thought he was spying on him, following him. The man didn't want that. He idolized Hoffa, affectionately calling him the "little guy," as did many of Hoffa's aides.

Hoffa was, in fact, smaller than most of the men he surrounded himself with. He controlled them by being a master of verbal abuse and by setting up ways to make them fear him.

Just as an exasperated, impatient Hoffa was ready to get into his car and go home, this eye-witness said a black, four-door Ford LTD drove in front of it.

Inside were a driver and two other men who looked to this witness's practiced eye like federal marshals or agents. The two passengers got out of their Ford and pulled what looked like identi-fication badges from their pockets. The witness said they spoke briefly with Hoffa. He assumed they were telling him who they were, that they had a few questions and would he please come with them.

This happened all the time, the witness said. Hoffa was used to it. He did what he usually did. He quietly got into the backseat with the two men, and the car drove off.

The witness followed behind them on a road that led straight to the Pontiac airport. Then he turned off to go on to his meeting in Flint.

Later, when this witness heard about Hoffa's disappearance, he wondered if the federal agents had had a plane waiting for Hoffa in Pontiac, if they had gotten rid of him in one of the big, deep lakes within easy flying distance — Lakes Michigan, Huron, and Superior.

No one, he added, ever looked into that. No one ever tried to find out if any private planes left Pontiac that afternoon. And no mention of the federal observers who had filmed Hoffa's life since his release from prison was included in the official report of his last day.

If that is indeed what happened to Jimmy Hoffa on July 30, 1975, then the federal government had taken a page from Hoffa's own book.

Hoffa firmly believed that one ruled through fear, and that the ends always justified the means. That attitude was embedded in the instructions he always gave his aides: "Do what you have to do in order to survive."

Had Jimmy Hoffa disappeared as part of a government plot?

Or was his disappearance the result of an underworld scheme to get rid of him?

Were whatever schemes or plots to get rid of him undertaken with the knowledge and approval of other Teamsters Union leaders? Had these leaders feared the "little guy" might be able to resume leadership of the union?

It's highly probable that no one will ever know for sure.

The waters around the Jimmy Hoffa case are very murky, and they're patrolled by killer sharks.

For what it's worth, however, the man the government named as Hoffa's actual killer, Salvatore Briguglio, was shot to death months after Hoffa's disappearance. He was standing outside a New York City restaurant when he was killed in a gangland-style revenge killing.

At the Teamsters International convention in Las Vegas in May 1986, a resolution was introduced to take Jimmy Hoffa's name off the union records. The resolution would strike his status as president emeritus, a term that would have been used if he had retired. The resolution was defeated by chanting delegates: "As long as there's Teamsters, there'll always be Hoffa. As long as there's Teamsters, there'll always be Hoffa."

Hoffa had always done what he had to do in order to survive, just as he told his associates to do. In a peculiar way, he *had* survived.

Richard Colvin Cox

On the night that he mysteriously vanished in January 1950, Richard Colvin Cox was in his third-class year at the United States Military Academy, West Point. He was, in civilian words, a sophomore. His disappearance is one of the most famous missing persons cases of modern times.

It was astonishing because Cox was a model cadet. Yet he had broken the rules of the highly regimented academy by going AWOL (absent without leave). And, if information gained by exhaustive searches is true, Cox had managed to go AWOL while still *inside* the grounds of the Point!

There is probably no other place on Earth that Richard Colvin Cox would have wanted to vanish from less than the Point. He had worked long and hard to get there.

A native of Mansfield, Ohio, Cox had graduated from high school with an excellent record. He enlisted in the army in 1946 and was assigned to duty with the 27th Constabulary Squadron stationed in Germany. He intended to gain admission to the Point as recommended "regular army."

Cox's excellent high school record was mirrored by an excellent record as a soldier. He worked hard, earning top-rated performance marks and rising to the rank of sergeant. When his superiors recommended him for the competitive army examinations for West Point, Cox took them.

His achievement record was unblemished by his test scores. He earned both a superior grade and his long-cherished appointment to the academy.

Meanwhile, his mother had also been working on securing that appointment. She had gained her son a recommendation from an Ohio congressman. One way or another, Richard Colvin Cox's determination to attend West Point would be fulfilled.

He entered the academy as a fourth-class cadet in June 1948. He had already served time as regular army, so his first day wasn't as overwhelming as it was for others in the incoming class. If other fourth-class cadets were shocked to discover that they were "expected to produce phenomenal results in a single afternoon," as the West Point catalog puts it, Cox wasn't. He eagerly started the six-week basic training program.

Cox already knew much of what that program was about. He knew traditional military courtesy. He knew how to "wear the uniform," how to keep his room in inspection-ready condition, how to march in parades. He was familiar with the physical exercise designed to whip cadets into shape for the real world of the military. He was familiar with long foot marches, rappelling down rock faces, and all the rest. He was familiar with rifles and tactical maneuvers. He knew he would be expected to respond quickly and accurately to his commander, even when he was under mental and physical stress.

Still, this was West Point — the answer to Cox's longtime dream. Even a regular army man like Cox, who had lived the life of a recruit, could expect a little stress on entering the academy. There was more at stake now.

But Cox handled that stress beautifully, too. He finished the initial six-week training period, and he and the other successful cadets were formally accepted into the United States Corps of Cadets in mid-August.

At the end of the full-dress parade acceptance ceremony, Cox and the other members of the fourth class — the Plebes — were assigned to one of the companies that make up the corps.

The rest of his Plebe year, Cox spent the same way his fellow cadets did — studying military heritage, standards of professional behavior, small unit tactics, and map reading. He completed still more physical training. By the end of May, Cox and the other Plebes had won the recognition of being upper-class cadets.

After a June vacation, the work went on and so did Cox. He stood in the top third of his class. He was good in military science, and he was a good athlete, joining the track team and becoming one of the Point's best long-distance runners.

In short, Cox demonstrated that he had what it takes to be a model West Point cadet.

Cox had become what he'd wanted to be. He was a part of the "long gray line" of cadets proud of their profession and dedicated to "Duty, Honor, Country." He believed in the rigorous self-discipline that the Point required. He saw value in the academy's moment-to-moment control of a cadet's life. He signed in and out for specific destinations at the academy checkpoints, without hesitation or irritation. He saw no reason that academy authorities shouldn't know where he was at any given moment.

Cox followed the rules, signing in and out, studying, rolling his mattress and bedding each day, and all the rest of it. And on January 7, 1950, Cox was still following academy rules.

Those rules, however, couldn't — and didn't — keep out disruptions and intrusions from the world beyond West Point. And, looked at with hindsight, serious disruptions and intrusions *were* plaguing Cox.

The first inkling of them was fielded by Cadet Peter Hains, Charge of Quarters, B Company. He took a phone call from a man who asked if a Dick Cox was in Hains's company. Hains told him there was. The caller said to tell Cox that "George, who served with him in Germany, is here." Hains was pretty sure the man on the other end of the telephone line had said his name was George, but he wasn't positive.

Hains told Cox to expect a visitor, noticing that

Cox seemed a little puzzled when he heard about the message. "I have no idea who that could be," Cox said.

When he met the man at five-thirty that night in Grant Hall, however, Cox recognized his visitor. Officer of the Guard in the hall, a large room used for guests, was Cadet Mauro Maresca. He noted that Cox behaved as if he knew "George." Maresca later told investigators that Cox and the visitor shook hands and talked for a few minutes. They seemed glad to see each other, Maresca said later. "George" even kidded Cox about how he looked in his uniform when the two walked to the coat rack so that Cox could put on his coat.

Even though that meeting appeared to be friendly, Cox never referred to his visitor by name. Oddly, he called him "that man" or "my friend" instead.

Hains had heard "George's" voice, but Maresca was the only person who got a good look at him. Maresca told investigators that the mysterious visitor was relatively tall, just under six feet. He weighed about 185 pounds, and he had fair hair and a light complexion. He was wearing a trenchcoat.

Cox signed out for DP — dinner privilege — and he and the man left the hall. The only place to eat other then the cadets' mess hall was the Hotel Thayer, just inside the south gate of the academy.

He returned by seven that night and started studying, only to fall asleep over his books.

Cox's roommates decided to play a practical joke by taking a snapshot of him when the bugle call, tattoo, sounded at nine. Bugle calls tell military personnel the time and tell it loudly enough that no one could fail to hear, not even a West Point cadet asleep over his books.

The bugle call came right on schedule, startling Cox awake. His roommates' snapshot caught him that way. Only seven days later, Cox would vanish, and investigators were happy to have a recent photo of the cadet as they searched for him.

Cox's behavior immediately after he'd been shocked awake by the sound of the bugle was intriguing. He leapt up and ran into the hallway, shouting what sounded like "Alice!" One of his roommates asked about it when Cox came back into the room, but Cox didn't answer. Instead, he went to his neat bedroll, unrolled it, and dropped on top of it without bothering to undress or pull up the blanket.

Later, investigators asked Cox's roommates about what the cadet had shouted when the tattoo call startled him awake. Neither of them were sure. Cox may have shouted "Alice!" or he may have shouted *"Alles kaput,"* a German phrase that means "All is ended."

There may seem to be a large number of West Point cadets with bad hearing problems at this stage of the story. But, of course, the cadets around Cox were busy meeting their own strenuous routines. Which of them could have anticipated what happened next?

For about a week after that, nothing much *did* happen.

Cox followed the routine, living the regimented life of the Point. He didn't seem nervous or apprehensive or fearful. His grades didn't suffer. The only thing he said about "George" was that he hoped "he wouldn't have to see that fellow again."

But Cox did see him again. For some reason, he met "George" the Saturday after their first meeting.

They met on January 14, at 5 P.M., close by Cox's barracks. An hour later, after he had returned to his room, Cox told one roommate that he was meeting "George" again that evening for dinner. He'd already signed out for DP. He said that he didn't like the guy. "George" was "eccentric," Cox said, and he was ruining study hours.

So why meet "George" for dinner?

One roommate said he figured Cox had gone with "George" because he was looking for a way to eat a meal at the hotel instead of in the cadets' mess hall.

Cox's roommate listened to him, checked his watch, and began leaving the room. He glanced back. He said later that Cox was buttoning his long, gray overcoat, looking "kind of lackadaisical." The time was 6:18 P.M.

No one ever saw Cox again. He was buttoning his coat one minute, preparing to meet a man he said he didn't like for a dinner he may or may not have wanted, and lost forever the next.

No one ever saw Cox again, which is odd in the fishbowl world of the Point. No one saw Cox leave the barracks. No one saw him walk to the Hotel Thayer. There's no record of Cox having dined there, with or without "George."

What, then, happened to Cox? Had he and "George" gone somewhere else to eat?

Perhaps and perhaps not.

No one saw Cox go through the gate, and there were sentries guarding it. There was no record of anyone who looked like "George" driving away from the academy.

In fact, no one would have thought of keeping an eagle eye out for Richard Colvin Cox's whereabouts until many hours later. He was, after all, a model cadet. He had his act together, and he followed the rules.

Even when Cox didn't return by the regular 11:00 P.M. check-in time that night, no one was alarmed. It was Saturday, and cadets had a little leeway on the check-in time on Saturday nights. The duty officer overlooked Cox's absence.

But it wasn't possible to overlook his absence the next morning. Cox's roommates reported it to their tactical officer. This officer is charged with being the leader, supervisor, and counselor to the 110 or so cadets in each of the 36 cadet companies.

Once that report was made, the search for Cox took shape rapidly. The New York State Police were called in. A thirteen-state alarm was sent out. The C.I.D. (Criminal Investigation Division, a branch of the regular army) entered the case. In three days' time, public appeals for information on Cox were widespread.

At the same time, an intensive search began on the grounds of West Point itself. If neither Cox nor his companion had been seen leaving them, it stood to reason that one or the other or both might still be there. Even finding the remains of one or the other or both would shed some light on the mystery.

This search went on for two months. Dozens of regular army soldiers poured in. They went over cellars and attics in every building on the post and over the entire grounds. Delafield Pond was completely drained. Helicopters patrolled overhead day and night.

No trace of Richard Colvin Cox was found.

Leads about his whereabouts came to the C.I.D., a record number of them. Cox, they said, had been seen in hotel lobbies; in a Brooklyn, New York, swimming pool; in an Atlanta, Georgia, bus terminal and so on. All the leads proved false.

The search for "George" was equally frustrating. C.I.D. checked back through years of muster rolls of Ranger battalions. Their idea was that "George" might have abducted Cox or done away with him in some fashion. Cox, after all, had called the man "eccentric" and had shared shocking stories of the man's violent exploits with roommates. But no trace of "George" was ever found, either.

What really happened to Richard Colvin Cox?

No one knows.

He was in great physical shape. It would have been difficult for a single person to overpower him in order to either kill or abduct him. No ransom note ever materialized, although the Cox family wasn't wealthy, so there would be little point in anyone's holding him for ransom. And no trace of his remains, which would prove his death, were found during the army's exhaustive search of the West Point grounds or in the searches conducted in the surrounding states.

Had Cox simply run away? Had he broken under the double pressure caused by the daily stress of the academy's expectations and the sudden disruption caused by "George"?

Probably not.

Cox's grades were in as good shape as he himself was, and they hadn't deteriorated when "George" came on the scene. Besides, Cox was at West Point, where he had wanted to be for a long time. There was simply no apparent reason for him to run away.

So what happened to Richard Colvin Cox on January 14, 1950, after he stood in the alcove by his bed, buttoning up his long, gray overcoat and looking "lackadaisical"?

We can only be sure that Cox had duly signed out for dinner privilege, that it is the longest dinner privilege any West Point cadet has ever taken, and that he was lost . . . and never found.

Solved?

Sometimes missing persons *are* found . . . but mystery still surrounds their cases. Here are some more short tales of missing persons whose case files are closed, but not fully explained.

One such case was that of Harold Goldberg of Sedalia, Missouri. He disappeared in January 1974. Asked to identify a decomposed corpse as his body, his wife noted a scar, a bent finger, and missing teeth. On the basis of these, she said the corpse was her husband. The man was declared dead, and the corpse was buried.

Then, several years later, on November 7, 1976, Goldberg called his wife to tell her he was alive and well. He said he was running a restaurant in the Ozark Mountains and that he had had amnesia — a sudden lack of memory.

Goldberg's phone call cleared up one mystery — the question of what had happened to him. But it didn't explain another. Whose body was buried in that Missouri grave? That mystery is still unexplained.

The homecomings of amnesia victims can be surprise visits to their own funerals, since missing persons can be declared legally dead after an absence of seven years. In fact, a few missing persons have turned up to astonish judges who were in the process of declaring them legally dead!

Other amnesia victims lose their memories so completely that when they are found, they can't quite believe they are who other people tell them they are.

Perhaps the psychics are the most intriguing finders of missing persons. Police often ask their assistance in puzzling cases, but the psychics' ability to solve them is chancy. Peter Hurkos, a famous Dutch psychic, had helped police solve other baffling disappearances, but he struck out in the case of nineteen-year-old Robin Lee Reade of Lake Forest, Illinois.

Robin Lee disappeared on May 27, 1972, while on a trip to California and Hawaii. The two detectives her parents first hired were unsuccessful in finding her. Then her parents called in Hurkos. He took them on a far-ranging tour — to Oklahoma, Brazil, Argentina, and Hawaii — and pointed out several buildings in which he said their daughter was buried. But her remains *weren't* found until after the Reades hired Chicago private detective Anthony J. Pellicano in 1977.

Using standard investigative techniques, the detective found Robin Lee's grave on the side of a mountain outside Honolulu, Hawaii. Five years after she disappeared, Robin Lee's family finally knew where she was, if not exactly what had happened to her and why.

On the other hand, psychics sometimes have the last laugh on those using standard investigative techniques. The psychic's seemingly eerie knowledge turns out to be true.

The police of Lake George, New York, laughed at retired advertising executive Ted Kaufmann the first time he "map-dowsed" the location of two young men who had left home one winter night in 1981 to buy a quart of milk and never returned. They later found Kaufmann's dowsing was nothing to laugh at.

Dowsing is a method of using a divining rod or a pendulum to find underground water. Kaufmann, who'd never thought much about dowsing until he moved to his farm in New York's Adirondack Mountains, had gained a reputation for finding water — and missing persons — by first sitting on his porch and asking his pendulum questions.

When asked for help finding the missing men by the men's family and friends, Kaufmann accepted the challenge. He sat down to put a few questions to his pendulum. Were they alive? No. Had they been attacked? No. Did they have an accident with another vehicle? No. Were they near the village of Lake George? Yes. On the lake? No. *In* the lake? Yes. Did they drive the truck on the ice? Yes. (A winter ice carnival was in progress, and auto and other races were being run on the frozen lake.) Did the truck break through the ice? Yes. Was it in open water? No. On a pressure ridge? Yes.

Then Kaufmann "map-dowsed," working with his pendulum, a compass, and a map of the area. The truck, he felt, lay in Orcutt Bay in the lake. A visit to the site the next day pinpointed Kaufmann's sense that the truck was about one hundred and fifty feet from shore and in forty feet of water.

That's when police called Kaufmann in. They watched him go through the whole map-dowsing process in their offices, using a tourist map they gave him. They took notes, laughed as he left, and waited for the ice to break up. If the men had been trapped under the frozen surface of the lake, one or both of their bodies would rise after the spring thaw.

The ice broke up in April, and the body of one of the missing men rose to the surface. It drifted to shore about a mile from where Kaufmann said it would be.

Police called Kaufmann in again, this time taking him out in a boat. He dowsed for the truck. Anchors and buoys were tossed from the boat to mark the spot. The truck was later found — at a depth of thirty-nine feet and with an anchor in the back!

No one laughed this time, not even Kaufmann, who said, "Hard even for me to believe."

One missing persons case that's hard for *everybody* to believe is the case of Ada Constance Kent. She was a wealthy spinster who lived in a cottage in Whalebone Corner, England, from which she vanished in 1939. Over the years, police thoroughly searched the deserted cottage several times. No traces of Kent were found.

Then in 1949, ten years later, a bank asked a constable to take another look in the cottage. Kent had, mysteriously, made a deposit. Was she still alive? Was she planning to return home?

The constable searched the cottage one more time. What he found was astonishing. Whatever had happened to Ada Constance Kent resulted in her fully clothed skeleton sitting at a table beside a tray full of fresh food!

Had she turned up by herself? The questions raised in the case are still unanswered.

Sometimes the remains of a missing person are discovered in this shocking way. Other times, you have to be an expert who knows the whole story before you can even tell if you *have* discovered the remains of a missing person. One such case was reported in *Lost . . . and Never Found*. What, many people asked, had really happened to Michael Rockefeller?

Michael was the son of Nelson Rockefeller, who would later become the Vice President of the United States. He had vanished during a trip through Oceania, a series of South Sea Islands that includes New Guinea. He was collecting artifacts for a museum. Sounds tame enough. But when he didn't come home, questions arose.

Then in 1977, filmmaker Lorne Blai reported

events that indicated Rockefeller had been killed by the Asmat tribe of New Guinea. Further, and even more unsettling, he said that Rockefeller had been eaten by a member of this tribe of headhunters. This sounded crazy to many people. After all, cannibalism, the eating of other people, had long been made illegal by the Dutch government of the island.

Then Dr. Lyall Watson, a biologist and expedition leader, wrote a book published in 1987. He had lived with the Asmat and come to understand how they lived and thought. Their island isn't rich in land or food, but the Asmat and their neighboring tribes had found a way to balance their resources: For most of the people to survive, some had to die.

Those deaths weren't meaningless or random. No one went out and killed someone else just because he wanted a snack. Instead, this was serious business. A whole system had been set up to deal with it. The rules were complicated but balanced. They made sense . . . if you'd grown up in that world. Watson, an expert, saw conclusive evidence that Rockefeller had run afoul of some of the rules. According to Dr. Watson, the Asmat *had* killed and eaten him — and it all made sense from their point of view.

These cases of missing persons have been "solved," even though questions about them remain.

The cases of the other missing persons in this

book remain stories with *no* definite answers. Even after their families and those who knew and loved them are themselves dead, the questions nag at other curious persons.

Where did these people go? What happened to the ones who were lost . . . and never found?